IGNORANCE IS BLISS

"He's got a kind face and a nice cat. I think he ought to know."

"Billie Mae, you'll *hate* yourself in the morning."

"I don't care. I'm going to tell him."

By this time, I had already decided that I didn't want to know. "Why don't we all have another drink first?" I tried to break for the bar, but an iron hand caught my wrist and pulled me back. There was no sign of a velvet glove.

"It wasn't—" Billie Mae leaned forward, eyes boring into mine intently. "It wasn't an accident! In Zurich."

"That's all right." I tried, nervously, to pry the iron fingers from my wrist. "I know. I understand. It was suicide. It's too bad, but these things happen."

"No." What bothered me was that it was Winnie who answered. "No, it wasn't suicide."

That left . . . that left . . . I tried one last, hopeless toss of the dice. "Natural causes?"

"No!" They both spoke at once.

That left . . .

"Murder," Billie Mae said.

I hadn't really wanted to know.

"I thought you ought to know," Billie Mae said stubbornly.

"Thanks," I croaked weakly. If true, she had now made me an accessory after the fact. . . .

TOURISTS
ARE FOR
TRAPPING

MARIAN
BABSON

BANTAM BOOKS
NEW YORK • TORONTO • LONDON • SYDNEY • AUCKLAND

This edition contains the complete text
of the original hardcover edition.
NOT ONE WORD HAS BEEN OMITTED.

TOURISTS ARE FOR TRAPPING

A Bantam Crime Line Book / published by arrangement with
St. Martin's Press, Inc.

PRINTING HISTORY
St. Martin's Press edition published 1989
Bantam edition / June 1991

ISBN 0-553-29031-2

Published simultaneously in the United States and Canada

Bantam Books are published by Bantam Books, a division of
Bantam Doubleday Dell Publishing Group, Inc. Its trademark,
consisting of the words "Bantam Books" and the portrayal of a
rooster, is Registered in U.S. Patent and Trademark Office and
in other countries. Marca Registrada. Bantam Books, 666 Fifth
Avenue, New York, New York 10103.

PRINTED IN THE UNITED STATES OF AMERICA

RAD   0 9 8 7 6 5 4 3 2 1

TOURISTS
ARE FOR
TRAPPING

CHAPTER
ONE

I WAS LYING BACK COMFORTABLY, UP TO MY EARLOBES IN hot steaming water. Pandora was perched on the end of the tub, trying to catch droplets of water as they dripped from the tap. Now and then, just to keep her on her toes, I lobbed a few drops at her from my end of the tub. After all, even a Siamese cat ought to be conversant with the Facts of Life, public-relations style. Anyone can handle a smooth, steady job that follows a predictable course; it's the way you manage the things that come at you out of left field that shows how good you are.

Pandora was catching on pretty well. She kept her main attention on those tantalising drops welling slowly from the tap, but slanted a suspicious cross-eyed glare at me when she sensed any movement from my direction. She had just neatly batted a drop back at me when the telephone rang.

I stayed where I was, reminding myself that it was supposed to be a sign of strength of character not to leap to answer the telephone if it rang at an inconvenient moment. Anyone with anything urgent to communicate could ring again later. Besides, what were they doing ringing after midnight, anyway?

Then I remembered that my partner, Gerry, was out with his latest bird. A dizzy type who owned a badly dented white Lancia and drove like a drunken Grand Prix driver. How she retained her licence was a secret shared between her and a series of susceptible policemen—although, perhaps her bank manager had an inkling of it when he canceled her cheques. Someday, however, the law of averages was going to catch up with her—if no other law managed to—and, if anyone was with her at the time—

I lurched to my feet, sending a great tidal wave sloshing over the sides of the tub and nearly swamping Pandora. Cursing me briskly, she leaped for dry land. Pausing only to grab a towel, I followed her into the office.

When I turned on the desk light, I saw a trail of gleaming wet pawprints marching across the pile of envelopes waiting to be posted in the morning. They were all stamped, too.

"You did that deliberately," I accused.

She sneered at me from the far corner of the desk, defying me to prove it.

There was no time to argue. I snatched up the receiver with a twist of my wrist, so that the telephone cord went snaking across the desk at her. Cursing me again, she dropped to the floor and headed for the pantry. There was a wet triangular patch where she had been sitting. I was immediately contrite. She *was* awfully wet. "I'll dry you off in a minute," I promised.

"What was that? . . . Hello? . . . Hello?" the receiver was yammering at me.

"Perkins and Tate," I said quickly, recalled to order. "Good *morning*."

"Oh, Lord—it isn't!" the voice at the other end said dismally. "Oh, Lord—it is! I'm most terribly sorry. I hope I haven't got you out of bed."

"Not at all," I said nastily. "Pandora and I were just having a bath."

"Oh, Lord, I'm sorry, old man. I had no idea. I'll call back later."

"No, no," I said hastily (from the distraught tone of his voice, he'd interpret "later" literally and ring back in half an hour and succeed in getting me out of bed). "It's all right. Pandora's a cat."

"Most of them are," he said gloomily.

I took a deep breath. "Pandora is a cat," I said slowly and distinctly. "Four-legged variety. Siamese breed. You did not interrupt an erotic interlude. You did, however, drag me out of my bath, and I am soaking wet and freezing. If you have anything urgent—"

"No, no," he decided. "It's not *that* urgent. Morning will do. I'm terribly sorry. I've been working, and I lost all track of time. If you could be here first thing in the morning—"

"Where?" I asked quickly, before he could ring off.

"Oh, I'm sorry." He was in an apologetic rut. "This is Neil—Neil Larkin. You know, Larkin's Luxury Tours."

"I know," I said, placing the familiar voice now. We'd done the overseas publicity to launch Larkin's Luxury Tours earlier this year. They had seemed to be well under way, the usual moderate success, which could be depended upon to build up into an excellent business—if nothing untoward happened. It was a bit early for us to be hearing from them again. On form, they should only require booster shots of publicity in the spring and autumn to keep them ticking over nicely.

"What's the matter?" I asked, scenting a rat as easily as Pandora could.

"Lord!" he said simply. "Oh, Lord! I can't go into it now. Just be here in the morning. You'll meet Tour Seventy-nine then, and you can see for yourself."

"Tour Seventy-nine—?"

"There goes my other phone," he said. "It must be Zurich again. I'll have to ring off. I'll see you in the morning. Bring a camera."

"Neil, wait a minute—" But he had rung off.

I hung up the receiver reflectively and went to make my peace with Pandora.

When I arrived at the Bloomsbury office of Larkin's Luxury Tours, Neil was still on the telephone. Unshaven, haggard, and rumpled, with an ashtray overflowing with cigarette stubs and a thick miasma of smoke clouding the atmosphere so that you couldn't distinguish anything in the far corners of the room—he must have been here all night.

He finished the call and nodded to me. "Doug, sit down. I'll fill you in. Kate's gone to Victoria Station with the bus to meet them. We'll liaise at the hotel and I'll integrate you into the tour. Then, if you can go around with them for a few days, taking pictures we can send back to their local newspapers—maybe do a few jolly little stories about their adventures in England. You know, make it sound to the Folks Back Home like they're having a great time, and maybe, by the time they get home and read the stories and listen to their friends kidding them about the trip, they'll be convinced they had a great time, too."

"What kind of a time *are* they having?" That seemed to be the pertinent question, at the moment. Neil hadn't stayed up telephoning all night just for the fun of it.

"Well"—he was obviously trying to look on the bright side—"things could have been worse. I gather from the courier that it wasn't bad at all, until they got to Switzerland. They'd been enjoying themselves—a bit tired, maybe, but tourists expect that. And they knew they weren't being chivied about the way they might be on any other tour, because this was a Larkin's luxury tour, and you know our motto: 'Leisure is the last luxury.'"

I sat down, letting him ramble on. There must be a point, and presumably, he'd get to it sooner or later. His phone rang and he answered it absently, "Larkin's Luxury Tours," then stiffened.

"Here? Where?" His voice rose in panic, and he scrabbled frantically in an empty cigarette packet, trying to find a cigarette that wasn't there. I threw my own cigarettes across the desk to him.

"You *what?*" He took a deep breath and stretched his mouth into a smile shape. (If you smile on the telephone, so the theory goes, the smile will come across in your voice to the listener at the other end.) There was no smile anywhere else on his face. "No, no, that's quite all right. I quite agree. It was the only thing to do, in the circumstances. . . . Yes. . . . Yes . . ."

He lit the filter end of the cigarette and took a couple of deep drags before noticing it. He hurled it into the overflowing ashtray, where it smoldered vilely, and lit another one, taking greater care this time, although most of his attention was still centred on the telephone.

"Yes, I see. . . . Yes, of course. . . . Well, don't worry about it. We'll sort it out someway. And we'll get someone over to you at the hotel right away." (I didn't particularly like the look he threw in my direction as he said that.) "And the touring bus will be along as soon as we can get it there. You'll be back to normal just as soon as we can get you there."

He tucked the receiver between his shoulder and ear, still making assenting noises, and reached for a clipboard and a sheaf of papers. He tucked the papers under the clip and slid them across the desk to me.

I picked it up reluctantly. The top paper was headed "TOUR 79" and had a list of names under the heading. I stopped reading at that point. Instinctively I felt that this development boded no good for me.

"Yes . . . that's fine. Yes, I'll be along personally . . . with your English courier. By the way, how is—?" He pulled the receiver away from his ear and glared at it indignantly, then at me. "Those buggers hung up on me," he snarled.

"Too bad," I sympathised. "But remember, the customer is always right."

His brief glare reminded me that, at the moment, *he* was *my* customer. He pulled a desk drawer open savagely, snatched something out, and slammed it shut.

"They're *here*," he said. "Tour Seventy-nine. We've spent all night arranging passage on a private Channel yacht for them, but they didn't wait. They chartered a plane for themselves, and they're at the hotel now. Waiting."

"And Kate—whoever she is—is waiting at Victoria Station with the bus," I said.

"Precisely. I'll have to go and collect her." He ran his hand over his chin and seemed to realise for the first time that it was covered with stubble. "After I freshen up," he amended hastily.

"That's a good idea," I approved. "You might air this

place out, too—if you're planning to bring them back here, that is."

"No, I don't think we'll do that," he said quickly. "I think the best thing to do, in the circumstances, is to take them off on a tour immediately. The City of London Tour, I think. The trouble is"—he frowned—"they weren't due until next week. So the bus they should have had, the Luxury Cruiser, is still doing Scotland and the Lake District with Tour Forty-three."

"Ah, yes, the good old Luxury Cruiser," I reminisced. (We had held the press party in it—reclining seats for twenty, a private loo, and a fully equipped cocktail bar. "Blind Drunk Through Britain," we had christened the tours privately.) "How's it doing?"

"About thirty miles to the bottle." He grinned, then seemed to remember that it was no longer a laughing matter. "I wish we had it here now. It's just what we need for this tour. Instead, we've had to pull the old minibus back into service—and we're wide open to complaints—it's not the sort of thing we promised them in our advertising. We'll have to try to keep to short day trips in and around London until we can have the Luxury Cruiser. Of course," he sighed, "this crowd are going to complain, no matter what we do. They're bound to. Their trip's been ruined and— even though there's nobody they can really put the blame on—they'll blame us, just the same."

"What ruined it?" I might never get an answer, but I was still in there trying.

"What?" He looked at me blankly. "Don't you know? Oh, Lord—didn't I tell you?"

"No," I said. "And I'm all agog."

"It's unfortunate"—he shook his head—"but it's nobody's fault. These things happen. You just hope to hell they won't happen to any tour of yours, but every once in a while, they do. They're bound to. Sheer law of averages. She was elderly. She hadn't been well. Her goddamned doctor advised a nice trip abroad, the way the old-fashioned ones still do. It wasn't his fault, either, I suppose. Most of the time, it gives them a new lease on life. Either they love every minute of it, or else they're so damned miserable their one ambition in life is to get the hell out of Europe and go home where they can die in peace and comfort in their own beds."

"But this one didn't." I had caught the drift of his conversation and was way ahead of him. "This one died in—"

"Zurich. Last night—no"—he shook his head groggily—"night before last. They found her yesterday morning—nearer noon, actually. They thought she must be overtired and they'd let her sleep late. No one went to check up—it was only when a chambermaid got impatient that they found her. It was all very unfortunate."

I whistled softly. "Unfortunate" was an understatement. Tourists want to get away from it all. The whole point of foreign travel is that, no matter how uncomfortable, how exhausting, it's still "different." An exchange of the old familiar worries, if you like, for new and strange problems, which, at least, have the merit of novelty and recalled in tranquility at home, may even have their funny side and make good stories.

The last thing they want is to be slammed in the face with mortality. That isn't why they're paying premium prices for a luxury tour.

"And what's worse," Neil said, "she was one of the collegians."

"Collegians?" I had a sudden, disquieting vision of a

party of footballers and cheerleaders jogging around the Continent.

"Well, whatever you call them. They were a party from the same college town. They all knew each other, more or less. The other half of the tour came from all over; they didn't know any of each other before they met on the tour."

"I see what you mean," I said. It *did* make it worse. It meant one-half the tour was involved, more shaken and upset than the other half, who, while jarred and admitting the sadness of the incident, would still be resentful of the pall cast over their holiday and annoyed because the others were not so easily able to shake off the effect.

It was going to take more than a few pictures and sprightly stories in their hometown rags to convince any of them that they'd had a Fun Time. We were in real "Other than that, Mrs. Lincoln, how did you enjoy the play?" territory.

"I'm sorry about this, Doug." He came out from behind the desk and grabbed my lapel, stabbing at it with the other hand. "I hate to throw you in the deep end like this, but there's literally no one else to do it."

I looked down. The silver, lark-shaped badge glittered on my lapel. "Larkin's Luxury Tours. Courier."

"Now, wait a minute," I said. "I don't know anything about—"

"Just fill in for an hour or so," he pleaded. "Introduce yourself, chat them up, take some pictures. We'll get there as soon as possible. But I can't contact Kate yet, she'll be on her way to Victoria with the bus. I'll have to have her paged there in about an hour—that was when they were due in."

I picked up the clipboard with the papers and list of

names attached—I had known it boded no good. "Well," I said reluctantly, "as it's an emergency . . ."

"That's it!" Neil pounced on the word. "That's just what it is—an emergency! There may never be a bigger one. Lord, I hope not!" He had my arm, urging me toward the door.

"This is great of you, Doug, I really appreciate it. You shouldn't have any difficulty, they're all nice people. Just a bit upset."

CHAPTER
TWO

IT WASN'T ONE OF THE BLATANTLY LUXURIOUS HOTELS. IT WAS one of the small, tucked-away ones, where subtle elegance was a throwaway feature. There was no insistence on it. You were left to realise for yourself that you were reclining on a genuine Regency chaise longue, looking at your reflection in a Chinese Chippendale mirror flanked by Meissen wall sconces. The rooms didn't have desks, they had Carlton House writing tables, or davenports. The carpet might be Persian, Aubusson, or even Moorfields—you never knew your luck. Of course, if you didn't have some inkling of that luck, or tried pushing it too far, the management would very regretfully find that they were completely booked up at any future date you might wish to arrive. They can afford to choose their guests.

They were huddled together in the lobby when I arrived. Castaways, turning the usual hotel lounge arrangement of two sofas and two chairs into their own private, uneasy little island.

How long had they been here? I wondered. Since the telephone call to the office of Larkin's Luxury Tours? Were they that anxious to start on the tour of London? Or did they just want to be together for moral support, uneasy in the silences of their own rooms? Unhappy, in yet another strange country, not wanting too much time to think. After what had happened, who could blame them?

A tall, slightly stooped man with silver-gilt hair looked up and spotted the silver badge in my lapel. He said something to the others, got up, and hurried forward to meet me. I took a mental bet that this was Professor Tablor. (I had swotted up on the list of names in the taxi coming over.) Or was he too much the film typecasting of an academic? Perhaps the real Professor Tablor was the short, swarthy man talking to the dark, nervous-looking woman—who didn't look too happy about whatever he was saying.

The tall man stopped at close quarters and read my badge aloud. "Larkin's Luxury Tours. Courier." He dived for my hand, like a drowning man at a liferaft. "They told us you'd be coming for us," he said, pumping it up and down.

"My name is Douglas Per—" I began.

"Douggie. That's just great, Douggie. You come along and meet the folks now. You'll never know how glad they are to be where they can hear English spoken again. We're all sold on London already."

My arm in a modified hammerlock, he dragged me across the lobby. "I'm afraid you've all had a rather unfortunate time," I said. "It was a distressing thing to have happened."

"Yes, yes," he said. "But that seems like long ago now—and it was certainly in another country. . . . There's no point in dwelling on it. I'm sure we all want to forget. . . . We've been looking forward to our time in England. It's so pleasant to be where you can understand the language, and there can be no possible misunderstandings. I hope we didn't discommode you by arriving so early. After all that had happened, we felt we couldn't bear to stay on the Continent another minute. It seemed like the best idea to charter that plane and come straight here."

"Quite all right," I heard myself weakly echoing Neil Larkin. "We understand."

"Here we are, folks." The professor gave the effect of introducing me with a fanfare. "We're all set now. Here's Douggie to take care of us." I wondered again if he was the professor—or possibly some professional compere from American radio or television.

Eleven expressionless faces turned toward me. Eleven pairs of eyes stared blankly, almost with hostility, before the smooth practiced expressions of welcome slid over their faces.

"How do you do" . . . "Pleased to meet you" . . . "Hi" . . . the greetings mingled indistinguishably.

"Douggie, this is"—he waved a hand toward each of the group in turn—"Paula, Donna, Billie Mae, Winnie, Hortense, Horace, Sandra, John, Marie, Ben, Tony, and"—he beamed at me—"I'm Tris."

The bleak foreboding that had brushed against me when Neil pinned the courier's badge on me now settled down over me like a damp fog. It was going to be one of those days. Not a surname amongst them. I might have known it. Of course, they'd sort themselves out as the day wore on, but that wasn't much help at the moment. At least one thing was clear: I was right about the professor. There couldn't be two people named Tristan in Tour 79.

They began standing up, drawing their coats around them

in restless, expectant movements. They threw anxious little sidelong glances at me, waiting for me to take the lead. If only I could figure out what to do with them, I would. I mentally damned Neil thoroughly. *Chat them up*, he said. *For an hour or so, until we get there*.

In the first place, with the exception of Professor Tablor, they didn't seem to be the chatting kind. Apart from that, there was something vaguely wrong. My subconscious was giving out desperate signals, nearly swamped by the more immediate problem occupying the forefront of my brain. Like, what can I do with these characters for a whole hour, maybe more?

Somewhere amongst them, a stomach rumbled, and I had a sudden brainwave. "Have you eaten?" I asked. "Have you had yourselves a real, proper English breakfast yet?"

Several faces brightened hopefully, and I realised I was onto a good wicket. It's that five-hour time difference. Travel, say what you like, is tiring, anyway. So they adjust fairly rapidly—or think they do—to going to bed earlier, and the brightness of the day wakes them—or rather, reconciles them to the hour they're getting up. But that time clock in their middle can't be stilled so easily—it insists they're not hungry when a heavy meal is put in front of them, and it wakes them in the small hours to tell them they're starving. It doesn't take everyone the same way, of course. But in a group this size, you're bound to find someone ready to eat at any time.

"We had just a Continental breakfast at the airport," Professor Tablor said. "And that was hours ago—we left so early. I guess we could just about manage to force down some nourishment along about now, eh, folks?"

"Folks" murmured agreement, showing more animation

than I had yet seen. I began moving them toward the hotel dining room: it was the easiest and nearest eating place.

I stood in the doorway and automatically counted heads as they filed past me into the dining room and sorted themselves out into three companionable little parties of four. I looked at them, and a warning bell rang again. I checked the list on my clipboard, then went over to Professor Tablor's table. He seemed to be spokesman for the group, whether self-appointed or nominated by mutual consent, I didn't know.

"Aren't we missing someone?" I asked him. "According to my information"—I brandished the clipboard—"there should be another lady on this tour."

They looked at me blankly for a moment, and I had the sudden dread that I had put my foot in it. All four feet, in fact. Or someone at Neil's office had. Was it possible that the name of the dead woman had not been crossed off my list?

"Oh, you must mean Angie Hunt." It could only be one of the schoolteachers who spoke. A thin, not unpretty woman, with a strained look and a Midwestern twang in her voice. The taut faces of the others relaxed, the spectre at the feast dissolved. "It's all right. Angie has relatives here. She's gone to visit them."

"That's right," Tristan Tablor confirmed. "She has cousins in Edinburgh. She thought she'd like to spend this extra week with them, while the rest of us explore London, then join us again for the British Isles leg of the tour, as originally planned. As soon as we got into town, she went straight to King's Cross Station to catch the train. I put her into the taxi myself."

"That's right," the schoolteacher said, a bit defensively. "We thought it would be the best thing for her."

"Yes," Tristan Tablor sighed. "We didn't even try to persuade her to stay with us. We thought she'd be better off with her own people, under the circumstances. She was pretty upset. After all, she shared a room on the tour with Carrie . . . but she'd gone off by herself on a twenty-four-hour side trip that day. I suppose she thought, if she'd been there, she might have done something . . . helped . . . or it might not have happened at all. Nonsense, of course. *Che sarà, sarà,* as they said in Italy when Ben dropped his camera from the top of the Leaning Tower of Pisa." (But his face didn't match the attempted lightness of his tone.) "Nobody could have stopped or changed what was going to happen. But Angie took it pretty hard, just the same."

"I see." I wished I'd never brought the subject up. The two women at the table and the dark, swarthy man looked bitterly uncomfortable. We were getting side glances from the other tables, too, as though the others sensed that the conversation had taken a forbidden turning. I put on a bright, false smile for their benefit.

"Well, now"—I raised my voice as a waiter sauntered within range—"shall we order now? A real Olde Englishe breakfast. Bacon and eggs? Porridge? Kippers?" With relief I watched them reach for the menus and begin to debate the choices.

"Aren't you going to join us?" Professor Tablor asked. "I'm sure there's room for another chair at this table, if we all just move a little—" The others began hitching their chairs closer, making room for me.

"No, no, thank you," I said quickly. "That is, I'd love to. But I have a telephone call to make first. I'll join you as soon as I can. You go ahead and order. Don't wait for me."

I had a quiet cigarette in a deserted corner of the lobby and bribed a waiter to bring me a cup of coffee. Just to make an honest English gentleman of myself, I even stepped into the converted eighteenth-century sedan chair, which served as a telephone booth these days, and having bumped my head before getting the range of the ceiling, tried ringing the office. There was no answer. Gerry must still be out, and it was too early for Penny to have arrived to take up her secretarial duties. If only Pandora could be trained to answer the phone and take messages . . .

I had another cigarette and tried to persuade myself that no one would notice if I didn't appear for another half-hour. I didn't succeed, but I had an idea for relieving some of the strain. I went over to the newsstand and bought a well-assorted dozen morning newspapers, then returned to the dining room.

"Here we are," I said merrily, feeling like a Butlin redcoat of the early period, "your morning paper." I dealt them out, with fine impartiality, but made sure that no table got a duplicate. "You can't have a genuine English breakfast without a genuine English morning paper to read over it."

They caught at the papers thankfully, whether because they were starved for English-language news, or because they were prepared to enjoy the novelty—any novelty. Or perhaps—I tried to brush the thought away—because it saved them any further need to try to make conversation amongst themselves. From what I'd seen, as I came in, they'd been making heavy weather of it. Those who were trying at all, that is.

As they read, they cast curious glances at their neighbours' choices. It was one of those mornings when no major news was breaking, so each paper had opted for headlines featuring its own favourite trivia. It was enough to make any reader, let alone an unsuspecting tourist, wonder whether these papers were published in the same city.

I glanced over a shoulder at an inside page myself for a moment, my eye lighting on a critic's review of a nightclub performer. The critic opined that the singer was showing signs of maturity in his hoarseness—which was one of the least-actionable ways of insinuating "whiskey voice" that I had seen in a long time. Other than that, the paper looked fairly dull. The tourists, however, were lapping up the newsprint, even though the finer points of what they were reading were bound to escape them. If you're not born endowed with native cunning, it can take years to realise that "a man is helping the police with their enquiries" means "we think we've got the bleeder, boys." Or that "foul play is not suspected" is likely to indicate accident or suicide.

I decided not to enlighten them; they were doing fine by themselves now, reading out choice snippets of quaintness to each other. Those newspapers had certainly broken the ice. Leaving me with just one question. In a group that had been together for three solid weeks, why was there any ice still needed breaking?

Anyway, they were looking slightly happier now. Except, that is, for the ones who had ordered bacon. I should have remembered to warn them. Americans are accustomed to bacon sliced to paper thinness, "peeled," and crisped just this side of charring. To them, our thick slices, with the rind still on, warmed nearly to translucency in a frying pan, looked like slabs of uncooked unfamiliar meat.

They obviously felt rather like their fellow American who, when served with a blood-rare steak, remarked, "Hell, I've seen cows hurt worse than this get up and walk away." Maybe they didn't exactly expect the bacon to walk away, but it looked as though it might still have a few protesting "Oinks" left in it if they were rash enough to stab it with a fork. A grim certainty of trichinosis lurked in the dark corners of their minds.

I consoled myself with the thought that they had seemed to enjoy the eggs and had had enough sustenance to last them through until lunch. At which time, I must remember to warn them against the worst pitfalls of the menu. None of them looked hardy enough to face a trifle—at least, not the first day in England.

Meanwhile, I avoided the limpid, accusing eyes and glanced around the dining room. Which meant I was the first to spot the gleam of the silver lark on the collar of the slim girl in the doorway. Across the room, I could see the deep blue of her eyes, the pale porcelain of her skin, and the black Celtic drift of hair.

I rubbed my sleeve quickly over the silver of my own badge. This was a colleague to be proud of—and to claim as swiftly as possible. I started across the room toward her.

But Neil appeared in the doorway behind her. The possessiveness of his hand sliding along her arm told its story and made me remember the special quality in his voice when he mentioned "Kate."

Ah, well, I sighed, and continued walking toward them, you can't win 'em all.

". . . not one bloody word—" Neil broke off abruptly as I came up to them. "Here's Doug." A bright, unlikely smile lit his face. "I've told you about Doug. Doug, this is Kate. She usually works in the office, but she's stepping in as courier for this tour."

"Wonderful." I held out a hand to her. "Welcome aboard." With my other hand, I palmed my own badge and slipped it into my pocket. "Come over and I'll introduce you. Unless"—I glanced at Neil—"you want to do the honors."

"No, no, you go ahead." Still smiling improbably, Neil began backing away. "I have to get back to the office. I'm expecting an important telephone call. From Zurich. Any minute."

The gentleman was protesting too much. I raised an eyebrow at him, but he was immune to such subtleties. "You take care of Kate, Doug," he said, trustingly consigning her to me. "Fill her in on the details. I have to dash off now. I'll catch you up later—somewhere along the way. Jim is outside with the minibus—I've given him the route—I'll catch you up. After I've got that call through."

He beamed that bright, unbelievable smile at us again and backed through the doorway, leaving us grimacing uncertainly at each other.

"How do you do," she said, extending a tentative hand in my direction. "I'm Kathryn Lamb—of Larkin's Luxury Tours." (Just in case I had had any doubts about it.)

"How do you do." I took her hand, equally formal. "I'm Douglas Perkins, of Perkins and Tate (Public Relations) Limited."

That much established, we stood staring at each other in a friendly but impersonal manner. Something had to give, and it seemed to be up to me. "Would you like to meet the tour?" I suggested.

"Yes, please." I noted that she had a clipboard and sheaf of papers similar to mine. It might be instructive, sometime, to compare notes and make sure that they *were* the same.

"This way then." She seemed to draw upon inner reserves as we crossed the dining room, so that she was erect and confident as we approached the set of tables belonging to Tour 79.

Professor Tablor, as might have been expected, was the first to leap to his feet as we approached them. "We are honored! Honored, indeed, ma'am," he exclaimed, groping for Kate's hand. "Why, when we said good-bye to our pretty little Miss Margie in Zurich, we never thought we'd have such luck again. It certainly pays to travel with Larkin's Luxury Tours." His eyes rested greedily on her silver badge, and the territory surrounding it. "And your name is—?"

"Kate—Kathryn Lamb," she supplied, before I could say anything.

"Miss Katie," Professor Tablor said appreciatively, sliding an arm around her shoulders. "We just *know* you're going to take as good care of us here in England as our precious little Miss Margie did on the Continent."

(We all accepted the spirit of that remark and ignored the fact that a member of the tour had died, despite Miss Margie's good care.)

"Are we ready to leave?" Kate asked crisply. "The bus is waiting outside for the City of London Tour."

CHAPTER

THREE

AS THEY SORTED THEMSELVES INTO SEATS IN THE MINIBUS, the people of Tour 79 began to assume personalities. Kate stood by the door and ticked them off on her list as they boarded. I looked over her shoulder, matching the names to the passengers.

Paula Drayton and Donna Bately were mother and daughter, with a restless, disturbing aura about them that made me uneasy. Paula was an improbably glossy blonde, a divorcée—and not for the first time, judging from the fact that her daughter bore a different surname. They chose the front seat behind the driver.

The opposite front seat was immediately bagged by a gangling male adolescent—a situation accepted with obvious lack of enthusiasm by his mother. Mrs. Hortense Rogers, widow, and her son, Horace—that made two more Kate ticked off and I matched to the names on my list. The glamorous Mrs. Drayton and the small, slightly dumpy Mrs. Rogers smiled at each other across the aisle with patently false friendliness, and each mother made certain her teenager was firmly tucked into the window seat. That was fine. A Romeo-and-Juliet situation must have been all that Tour 79 lacked. No wonder so many were looking so worn.

The schoolteacher who had accounted for the missing tourist slid into the seat behind Donna. Her companion followed her, sitting behind Paula. That checked out Billie Mae Morgan and Winnie Holman.

"We'll have to *do* something about them," Kate murmured to me. "They weren't supposed to come to England at all. They're scheduled to fly back to the States at the end of the week. They were supposed to be in Paris this week."

We both looked at the schoolteachers, but they were settled into their seats with blank, expressionless faces. It was impossible to tell whether they resented the change in plans. Just in case, I'd get in a bit of extra PR work there.

The elderly couple introduced as John and Sandra took the seat behind the Rogerses'. They ticked off as Mr. and Mrs. Peters, the only married couple on the list. Obviously retired, and looking as though they wondered whether a European tour had really been the good idea it had seemed when they planned it. I wondered whether a few pictures in the hometown paper would convince them. Next time, they'd See America First.

The remaining woman, Mrs. Marie Manzetti, Professor Tablor, and the two men—Ben Varley and Tony Christopher—all chose window seats alone.

The professor smiled at Kate as she boarded the bus and stretched out one arm invitingly along the back of his seat. Kate smiled back benignly and settled herself into the little alcove made by the steps, beside the driver.

I walked down the aisle, smiling at everyone, and took the backseat, where I had room to spread out my camera gear. Also, I could keep watch over everyone from that vantage point and perhaps, spot the most potentially discontented. For a start, I spotted the professor waggling his fingers coyly at Kate. I decided it would be interesting to know what they called *him* on campus.

Kathryn Lamb picked up her hand mike and switched it on. Her voice echoed with metallic, faintly robotlike tones from the public address system. "Good morning, Tour Seventy-nine, and welcome to London. We'll begin our tour with the Houses of Parliament, Westminster Abbey, and the changing of the Guard—"

"Do you really need that thing, Miss Katie?" The voice cut across hers. "You've got such a pretty little voice. I'm sure it's strong enough to reach us all without the aid of that abomination."

"We'll try." She switched the mike off. "Can everyone hear me?" Murmurs of assent reached her and she replaced the mike in its holder.

The driver slipped the clutch into gear and the minibus moved smoothly into the line of traffic. "On your left, as we turn this next corner, you'll see . . ."

While Tour 79 lingered over morning coffee, I shared a peaceful cigarette at the kerbstone with Jim Davis, the little Cockney driver. At least, it was peaceful until Kathryn Lamb slipped away from the tour to join us. She accepted a cigarette from Jim and they exchanged a long look, then broke into the kind of cryptic shop talk designed to make my blood run cold.

"It isn't my imagination, Jim, is it?" .

"It isn't." He shook his head. "This little lot give *me* the ice-cold collywobbles. There's something dead wrong about them all."

"They've had a frightful time, of course." She was trying to rationalise, but I could see she was even more disquieted because Jim wasn't trying to laugh away her nerves. "They're probably still in a state of shock."

"They're in some kind of state, all right." Jim took a final drag on his cigarette and pitched it away. "Know what bothers me most? They don't talk—not even to each other. Did you ever see a bunch of Yanks that didn't chatter away like parrots in a jungle? I never did before. This lot just sit there. I keep getting the feeling that I want to turn around and look to see if they're still there."

"Perhaps it's the change of climate, change of water," I suggested hopefully. "They may liven up, now they've had their midmorning coffee."

"Take more than that to liven *them* up. A barrel of brandy, maybe. Then again, maybe not." Jim looked gloomily down the narrow street. "Here they come now. Not overfond of their own company, are they?" He turned and clambered back into the bus.

The bus moved forward, across Holborn Viaduct, to pass the Old Bailey. Jim slowed, so that they could look up and see the blindfolded statue of Justice on top of the building.

"And this is probably the most famous court in the world," Kathryn recited, a bit mechanically. "The Central Criminal Court, where lawbreakers are brought before the bar of justice . . ."

Without moving, the occupants of the bus gave the effect of withdrawing. Faces that had warmed into appreciation crossing the splendid Victorian excesses of Holborn Viaduct now closed. Eyes dulled, shoulders rubbed restlessly against the backs of seats.

At the front of the bus, Kate froze, with the panic of an actress losing her audience, but unable to tell what she had done wrong. Jim stepped on the accelerator and the Old Bailey slid away behind them. No one appeared to notice, but the atmosphere lightened.

From my seat, I could see Jim's lips move in the driving mirror as he muttered to Kate, "Let's speed it up and drop these bleeders early."

"We can't," she answered him soundlessly. "We're booked for the full afternoon tour—"

"Naughty, naughty," the voice we were beginning to recognize spoke up brightly. "No secrets. It's impolite. Besides, we're all friends here, aren't we?"

Kate raised her head and smiled blandly at Professor Tablor. "We are now approaching the Old Lady of Threadneedle Street—the famous Bank of England—"

"Are we supposed to be impressed by these old piles of junk all over the place?" Horace Rogers had decided to add the full weight of his seventeen years to the occasion. "I think it's all pretty stupid. If you want to know, it doesn't impress *me* at all."

"Now, Horace," his mother said fondly, "she's just doing her job."

"I'm sure *we're* very happy about it." Paula Drayton leaned forward, talking to Kate, but *at* Hortense Rogers. "I think any properly brought up young person ought to appreciate the finer things in life and the values of all those older generations."

"I can understand that." Hortense smiled in the adjusted driving mirror, a prim, precise, dangerous smile. "People who have never given their children a stable home life always feel strongly about history. As though it could make up for everything they've missed. But my late husband always used to say that there was no substitute for a father who came home every night. The *same* father every night, of course."

"Lumme," Jim muttered, "we've got *two* cats amongst these pigeons."

"Personally," Paula said, "I've always understood that *emotional* stability was more important than dull routine. When children know they're loved—"

Kate signaled frantically to Jim and the bus swept past St. Paul's Cathedral and down Ludgate Hill before she could get a word in edgewise—or perhaps she didn't want to.

The bus hurried down Fleet Street and came to an abrupt halt. "Lunch," Kate said hastily. "Just follow me across the street. We're having our lunch at Dr. Johnson's pub—the famous Cheshire Cheese."

Was there an imperceptible hesitation before they began to move? A cold drawing away from some unknown intangible that had suddenly been flung into their midst? Before I could analyse the abrupt change in atmosphere, Professor Tablor rose to his feet and took command.

"Did you hear that, folks?" he asked enthusiastically. "Dr. Johnson's pub! *Dr. Johnson's* pub," he repeated—he seemed to be taking it big. (Funny, for some reason, I'd have sworn literature wasn't his subject—but I could have been wrong. I often am.) "And *we're* going to eat there— won't *that* be something to write home about?"

They began to move, then. "Dr. Johnson's pub!" Little murmuring cries took up the rallying call. I'd no idea Dr. Johnson was such a popular folk figure back in the States. Perhaps it was some new fad.

They flowed across the street and up the dark alleyway

like a tidal wave. I splashed along in the rear, trying to convince myself that there were no undercurrents beneath the surface.

"Meet you back here in about an hour," I heard Jim tell Kate. "Won't be able to park. If you're not here, I'll keep circling until you come out."

She nodded to him and hurried to join me. There were lines of strain on her face that hadn't been there this morning. Well, no one had ever suggested that the tourist trade was an easy way to get rich quick. And this little lot gave every promise of being more difficult than most. Perhaps you couldn't blame them for it—but it didn't make it any easier for those who had to deal with them.

I'd hoped that we couriers might be able to sit at some side table away from the main group; but no, they had saved places for us at the long table. It was the kind of thoughtfulness I felt I could do without. From her strained smile, Kate, too, would have preferred a brief respite from the job. It was not to be, however, and there was nothing for it but to bite the bullet.

This time, mindful of my duty, I gave a strong lead by plumping heavily for the steak-and-kidney pie. Trustingly, they followed me. I left them to their own devices for the first course, and pleading the necessity of an urgent telephone call, I avoided the Brown Windsor soup. As I went, I heard Kate beginning a long and chatty exposition on Dr. Johnson, his life, work, and pubs. She sounded as though she had done her homework extremely well. I made a mental note to tender warmest congratulations to Neil: If all the guides were as good as she was, Larkin's Luxury Tours would put him into the luxury bracket himself very shortly.

In the telephone booth, I rang the office number again. It

was still too early for Penny to be there, but Gerry ought to be back by this time. He ought to be.

I heard the phone ringing monotonously at the other end. Just as I was about to hang up, there was a sudden clatter and I was through to the office. He must have just come through the door.

"Gerry?" I said. "Gerry?"

"Prryow?" an obliging little voice commented at the other end of the line.

"Gerry? Are you there?"

"Prreh?" There was a strange sliding, thudding sound, as though an ear were being rubbed against a receiver slipping out of reach.

"Pandora," I yelled, "I can't talk to you—hang up!" Then, of course, I realised that she couldn't—even if she'd understood and wanted to.

I leaned weakly against the side of the telephone kiosk and cursed the well-known Perkins luck. A fine thing—I had a partner out on the tiles, and a domesticated cat who answered the telephone. Somewhere, there must be a happy medium!

A resounding clatter jerked me upright again. The receiver must have slipped off the desk. A steady thumping told me it was swinging against the side of the desk. Or perhaps Pandora had leaped to the floor and was playing with it. Now that I came to think of it, there was a certain lack of playthings for her. Perhaps I ought to see if the funds could run to a catnip mouse or something.

An uneven clatter, interposed with little hunting cries, told me my guess was correct—she was playing with the swinging receiver. I hung up wearily. There was nothing I could do about it. When Penny or Gerry arrived, they could deal with the situation. I wondered, with brief amusement,

what Pandora would do if British Telecom put the screamer
on the line to signal the receiver needed replacing. She
didn't like loud noises. It would annoy her intensely. . . .

Back at the Cheshire Cheese, the steak-and-kidney pie
had arrived and been dealt out. Tour 79 was tucking into it
with every evidence of enjoyment—they were nearly finished.

The same couldn't be said for Kathryn Lamb. Her plate
looked almost untouched, and she was still talking, with a
trace of desperation in her tone, about Dr. Johnson and his
circle. Tour 79 appeared to be hanging on her words and
encouraged her with murmurs of interest whenever she
seemed to be flagging. She looked as though she could have
done with a less appreciative audience; but I wondered
whether they were really so interested in the Johnson circle,
or whether a running commentary throughout the meal was
desirable to them because it saved them from having to
make polite conversation with each other.

I hurriedly gulped down my own meal, preparatory to
taking over from her for the dessert course. I might not know
much about Dr. Johnson, but some time in the States had
taught me quite a bit about Americans. One way or another,
I felt I could hold this audience as well as she could and
give her a chance to rest her voice. She still had the
afternoon tour to talk through.

Down at the other end of the table, they were already
reaching for the menu again, while the waiter began clearing
away their plates. A couple of them lit cigarettes, but I
decided not to say anything. What the hell, we weren't going
to have a toast to the Queen, anyway.

Kate paused to take a couple of mouthfuls and a neutral
debate on the merits of the respective desserts broke out
cautiously at the end of the table. I decided to put a word in
for an Olde Englishe favourite.

"I'd like to recommend the Stilton," I said.

Everyone stopped talking. Faces turned toward me, blank, unbelieving. Once again I had the sensation of having tripped over a step that wasn't there. They couldn't have understood me. Heaven knows what they thought I'd said. I ran hurriedly over my somewhat dated stock of American slang obscenities. Unless something new had been added, I was in the clear there. But they still looked distinctly shocked.

"Stilton cheese," I elucidated. "One of the finest English cheeses. I always feel that there's nothing to round off a meal like crackers and Stilton cheese."

Hortense Rogers screamed abruptly. She threw down her napkin and still screaming, pushed back her chair so violently it toppled over.

"How could you?" she flung at me. "How could you?" And burst into sobs.

The schoolteachers fixed me with somber accusing looks, then rose and advanced on Hortense. One on each side, they bore her off to the ladies' room.

What had I said? I went back over the words. They were completely innocuous. At least, so far as I knew. Certainly there had been nothing in them to cause this reaction. Was it something I had done?

Kathryn Lamb rose quickly and followed the women out of the dining room. Her backward look at me was harassed, but frankly puzzled. So, she didn't know, either.

In the embarrassed silence, no one seemed ready to enlighten me. Some of the tour had already retreated behind the menu again.

I found I had lost my appetite. Also any desire to be helpful. "All right," I said bitterly. "*have* the trifle, then!" That would teach them.

I pushed back my own chair and stood up. No one made any move to stop me. "You'll excuse me, I'm sure," I said.

Out of the corner of my eye, I was aware of Young Horace slipping quietly out of his seat. There seemed to be a nasty glint in his eye. I moved a bit more quickly, just in case he had any notions about chivalry and the need to avenge his mother's honour. I was in no mood for duels—especially when I didn't even know what I had done.

I was nearly out of the door when a heavy hand fell on my shoulder.

"Son," Professor Tablor drawled, "I think it's high time you and me had a little talk." The hand pushed me firmly through the doorway.

CHAPTER
FOUR

THE RELENTLESS HAND ON MY SHOULDER PROPELLED ME ON-
ward; down the stairs, out the door, down the alley, down
Fleet Street, up a side turning, until—finally—we were
sitting in a little hole-in-the-wall coffee shop, with cups of
coffee in front of us. Professor Tablor—I didn't feel like
calling him Tris at the moment—faced me across the table
with the sort of expression I hadn't seen since the days
when I used to be ushered into the headmaster's study.
Perhaps it was an occupational hazard with teachers—their
faces automatically fell into such a mask when they were
called upon to be serious, but it didn't make me feel any
better. My iniquities were about to be pointed out to me—in
gory detail. All that would be missing would be the proph-
ecy of what would become of me once I left the shelter-
ing and understanding halls of ivy. On second thought—I
glanced at his face again—I might get that, too. I was

obviously fated to come to no good end. The fact that I was in public relations would undoubtedly signal to any headmaster type that I was already well on the skids. There were days when I felt that way about it myself—and this was one of them.

Professor Tablor cleared his throat and spoke in slow, measured cadences. "Hortense," he said, "is a very sensitive woman. She has been on the Board of Governors for many years now; and I, personally, have dealt with her, man and boy, across more than twenty years. She is a *very* sensitive woman."

There was no arguing with that one. Unless I wanted to take the position that he was putting it too mildly. So far as I could see, Hortense was a shrieking neurotic. I nodded.

"Mind you," he went on thoughtfully, "I blame myself."

I decided I wouldn't even try to analyse that one. I just waited.

"She seemed so much better. She even mentioned that she'd stopped taking them, and I was very pleased about it, because she couldn't have gone on the way she was going I thought—" He brought his hands up and seemed about to bury his face in them. At the last moment he looked at them in surprise and lowered them again helplessly. "I thought the trip was working."

"I see," I said carefully. "But should we just be sitting here? Now that she's had another of her . . . um . . . turns, oughtn't we to get her to a doctor, or something?"

"A doctor?" He raised his head and stared at me in amazement. "Son, what are you talking about?"

"Hortense Rogers," I said uncertainly. "Weren't you?"

"Hortense?—never!" he said. "Why should I be? Why

there's nothing wrong with Hortense. Apart from her being so sensitive, that is. No, I was talking about Carrie."

"Carrie?" I ran my mind back over the list. There was no Carrie on it. But—

"Poor, dear Carrie." He dipped his head in tribute. "She was a good woman, and a wonderful teacher, but she got too involved with her students."

It was clearer now. "Carrie is"—there must be a delicate way of wording this—"the one you . . . left behind in Switzerland?"

He nodded. "That's Carrie." He paused and corrected himself. "That *was* Carrie."

"I'm sorry," I said. It seemed as adequate a comment as any.

"We were *all* sorry." He sighed heavily. "Poor Carrie hadn't been having an easy passage lately. There was a serious incident . . . a tragedy, really . . . at the college last year. Involving a student. A young man . . . only twenty-three—"

There was time for several lurid speculations about lady teachers and young male students to race through my mind before he spoke again.

"He was a good student—not as brilliant as she thought he was, not by any means—but difficult. Very difficult. I know, because he was one of my students, too. Carrie had him for English literature, and I teach chemistry and physics. Mind you, I supported her in the fight when the board wanted to expel him. After all, he'd been to Vietnam before coming to college—it does things to them. Not that some of our hometown kids, who'd never been farther away than New York, didn't smoke pot, too. But you can't expel them all—not these days. And the board were all for making an example of someone who wouldn't cause any local controversy. Peter fitted the bill, especially as he was so *noisy* about everything."

"So, they expelled him," I said, "and it upset her."

"No," he said, "it never came to that. Before we'd finished arguing the matter, Peter committed suicide. Carrie discovered the body, hanging from the shower rail in his room. She went round when he missed a class—thought perhaps he was sick, or drugged—she was always covering for him. And of course, he needed extra protection with the Board of Governors on the rampage."

He was shaking his head, and I shook mine. "That's too bad," I said. "That she should have discovered him. That was really unfortunate."

"It was," he said. "She got the fixation that it was all her fault, that she had failed him in some way. It was nonsense, of course. Why, it would have been as sensible to have blamed me. I probably upset him more than she'd ever done. When they're so delicately balanced, you never know what slight push might send them over the edge. And I had to tell him he wasn't as brilliant as he thought he was. That that formula he was ranting about had been discovered and discarded years ago." We shook heads again. "They never want to believe that they can be following in older footsteps, especially unsuccessful ones. If anything sent Peter off, it was far more likely that than anything Carrie might have said or done."

"Terrible," I said, remembering a couple of fellow students at Harvard School of Business Administration who'd been deeply shocked and upset to learn that their theories on strike-breaking techniques had been tried in the last century by the robber barons and subsequently outlawed by the Supreme Court. "I suppose you must see a lot of that sort of thing in the course of a few academic years?"

"More than you'd think," he said. "Lots of it gets hushed up. The more thoughtful ones manage something that can be passed off as an accident to their parents. Some of them may even contrive to get themselves murdered—going around stirring up trouble, asking for it until they get it—and then the blame is put on someone else. And some of them are so ambiguous that we can never be sure ourselves. You have to grow a tough protective hide about it, if you want to carry on as a teacher. You evolve your own philosophy about it. Me, I've figured that there are just people who are survivors, and people who aren't. Some of them almost seem to be looking for any excuse to finish it. Others come through events that would poleax an elephant—they may not come through smiling, or even fighting, but they come through.

"Generally, I've always put the dividing line at about the age of thirty. Funny, but it's mainly the young ones who can't face life—or whatever they think life is going to be. But if they reach thirty, they're going to go on. They're the survivors. By that time, life has thrown enough at them to make them give it up, if they're going to. They've had all the excuses they need. And they haven't taken them. They've learned to live with their own shortcomings, and with other people's. They're the survivors."

"You've given the matter a lot of thought." He'd have to have done, of course. It must hit them hard, the first couple of kids they lose that way. They have to give up themselves then, or else work out their own way of coping with it. "I think you're very probably right."

"I'd thought I was." He had finished his coffee without noticing it, and now he stared into the empty cup as though the grainy dregs had a message for him. "I was sure of it.

But Carrie was well over thirty—well over forty, in fact. And she committed suicide."

So that was the reason for the strange atmosphere surrounding Tour 79. It was the miasma of guilt, doubt, and unease emanating from those left behind. Those wondering, Could I have done something to prevent it? Was it I who failed, and where? How?

"That's terrible," I said, wishing to hell I had more information. Had she hung herself from the shower rail, like her pupil? Taken sleeping tablets? Cut her wrists? Who had discovered the body? I cursed Neil mentally, but he might not have had any answers to give me. He'd seemed quite thoroughly occupied on unsatisfactory telephone lines during most of the past twenty-four hours.

"Terrible," the professor agreed, nodding his head. He put down the coffee cup and faced me squarely. "Terrible."

We might be agreed, but we weren't getting very far. It seemed there was nothing for it but a direct question.

"How did she do it?"

"She . . ." He gave a deep sigh and raised his hands to his face again, in that abortive gesture. "She ate a cheese fondue."

I could not have heard that correctly. I stared at him, but he seemed unaware that he had suddenly lapsed into gibberish. "I beg your pardon?"

"She . . . ate . . . a . . . cheese . . . fondue," he repeated, slowly and distinctly. It still sounded the same to me. "The very last thing in the world she should have done. I should never have allowed it. But she told me it was all right, and I believed her. Like a fool, I believed her."

He looked up then and must have registered the glazed look in my eyes. I smiled weakly. "A cheese fondue?" I threw his own words back at him, hoping he might correct me.

"That's right," he said. "And she'd been warned. She'd been on those tranquilizers since all the upset last year. And the doctor had impressed it upon her particularly— cheese, of any sort, was deadly poison to her while she was taking those tranquilizers."

Americans and their goddamned pills! Better living through chemistry! Whatever happened to the good old-fashioned panacea of just getting drunk? You might wake up with a hell of a hangover in the morning—but at least you *did* wake up.

One thing, it certainly explained the reaction I got when I carelessly recommended the Stilton. Also the hesitation about going into anything named the Cheshire Cheese.

"But, a cheese fondue—" It still seemed incredible to me. I'd heard vaguely about a case or two, but one doesn't necessarily trust all newspaper reports. "Could it really do that?"

"It could be fatal—it *was* fatal." He leaned forward and stared at me earnestly. "I don't know how much information you have about us in that private file of yours." His eyes rested greedily on the sheaf of papers attached to the clipboard. (I put my hand over it defensively, in case he might be going to snatch it away to prove some point. I didn't know how much private information it contained, either. I'd spent most of my time trying to memorize names and match them up with their owners.)

"I don't know, for instance"—he gave a faint sigh, perhaps relinquishing, if he had ever held it, the idea of taking the file from me—"whether it tells you that I'm a diabetic. Oh, it's very well controlled, and I'm very careful— not too noticeably, I hope. And it was the same with Carrie and her tranquilizers. She took them in private, and we had only her word for it that she'd stopped taking them as soon as she got to Europe. I was even pleased about it—I'd encouraged her to come on this tour. I'd hoped it would help her to forget—and it had seemed to be working. I was delighted.

"But the point I'm trying to make is this: Cheese was deadly to Carrie—and she knew it. For her to sit there and eat that cheese fondue was as much an act of suicide as it would be for me to eat my way through a box of chocolates. She knew what she was doing, and it was deliberate. And she'd lied to all of us, so that we sat there and let her do it. That's what's so awful about it. That's why we couldn't stay on the Continent another minute. I must say, the police were very kind and understanding about the situation. And your little courier lady was a tower of strength."

"Larkin's Luxury Tours employ only the best, most capable couriers," I said feebly. It was a line from the brochure, all I could remember, but it seemed to fit the situation.

He nodded agreement. If he remembered the line at all, he must really think me a company boy. Of course, he had no reason to think otherwise. We'd never been properly introduced or identified. So far as he was concerned, I was just another, supplementary courier.

"Perhaps we ought to rejoin the tour now," I suggested, taking up my clipboard. As we left the coffee shop, I made a mental note to check with Neil. If he'd scheduled a trip to Cheddar Gorge, we'd better scrub it.

I settled myself at the rear of the bus again, and the others all fell into the seats they had been occupying this morning. Evidently, there was no chummy switching around for private chats, or changing places for window seats on this tour. With the cloud hanging over them, perhaps it wasn't surprising. They probably weren't even thinking about such niceties. In their places, I doubted that I'd be. It occurred to me that there was an especially antisocial aspect to killing yourself while on holiday with a group of people. It was bad enough in the privacy of your own house, but it was infinitely worse when you managed it more or less in public, ruining the enjoyment of life for as many innocent bystanders as possible.

As Kathryn Lamb took up her spiel again and the bus wheeled smoothly into the Fleet Street traffic, I picked up the clipboard and began leafing through the papers at the back.

There was a separate page for each of them. It gave their full names and home addresses, and the name and address of the next of kin to be notified in case of emergency (*That* must have been useful in Switzerland, although I doubted that Neil had envisaged such a dire emergency.) Other than that, it simply listed whether or not the subject was a vegetarian, the religious affiliation (if any), and whether or not access to a place of worship must be provided on a particular day.

There was a blank section, hopefully captioned "Other Comments." Presumably, this was to have been filled in by their original Continental courier before she passed them on to her English colleague. Things being as they were, however, the Continental courier had had too many other things on her mind to worry about filling in small details relating to the physical comfort of her erstwhile charges.

It was interesting—and vaguely sinister—that no mention was made of Professor Tablor's diabetes. That being so, it was also dubious that there had been any notation on the

departed's information sheet warning that she must be kept
away from cheese in any form. I wondered uneasily how
many of the others ought to be receiving special attention
and had neglected to inform their courier of the fact. I
thought of penciling in the notation about Tablor myself, but
I shrank from marking the blank page. Perhaps he didn't
want it generally known—a lot of people didn't. He had it
under control and could take care of himself. Perhaps it
would be enough if I just quietly picked up the watching
brief.

Villiers Street slid past outside the bus just then, and
Trafalgar Square, and I was conscious of a great wave of
homesickness. I wanted to be back in the office flat on the
top floor of one of the buildings at the lower end, and doing
something constructive—like teaching Pandora to hang up
the phone; or better still, not to knock it off the hook in the
first place.

And perhaps Gerry had surfaced in the past hour or so.
Once I began to think of them, the reasons for an immediate
return to the office began to mount up. I'd taken a few
photographs during the morning, but the day had darkened
now and rain looked imminent. I hadn't brought any flashbulbs, so that took care of any more pictures.

Besides, I'd already seen Hampton Court. The mere
thought of Tour 79 struggling through the Maze in a soaking
downpour made me want to pull the communications cord
and cut and run.

Instead, I made my way to the front of the bus and had a
quiet word with Kate and Jim. They agreed that there was
nothing of value I could do at Hampton Court. They were off
duty themselves at six, when they dropped the tour back at
the hotel. The tour had a free evening—presumably they'd

gravitate to the theatres of their choice. We would all meet at the hotel again in the morning.

This being decided, Jim drew the bus in to the kerb and I waved a cheery good-bye to the tour and dismounted. Several people waved back as the bus drove off down King's Road. I was outside a supermarket, which was fortunate, as I'd been planning a certain amount of necessary shopping. I went inside.

Pandora was curled up on the desk when I let myself into the office. She rose and stretched, yawning a muffled greeting. The telephone receiver still hung over the side of the desk, buzzing gently. I put the bag of groceries down on the desk top while I retrieved the receiver and replaced it.

In that split second, Pandora dived into the bag with a happy cry. "There's nothing in there to interest you." I hauled her out, protesting vigorously. She didn't believe me—not for a moment. Everyone knew delicious tidbits were concealed in bags like that.

"All right," I said, "I'll prove it to you." I began to unpack: a loaf of bread, half pound of butter, half-dozen eggs, two small lunchbox-size tins—

"*Arr-yow-yow!*" She fell on them, glaring at me. She'd known I was lying to her.

"They're nothing to do with you," I said. "You wouldn't be interested."

"*Yrayrow!*" I was lying again. Everyone knew what came in small, interestingly shaped tins. Fish—that was what! Fish! And I was trying to keep it from her. Why? Why? There was another cat! I was two-timing her again!

Eyes narrowed, tail lashing, she paraded up and down the desk, berating me. She'd met my type before—any little alley cat that flirted her whiskers at me had me chasing after her. I was an unfaithful, weak-willed, simpleminded—. Her language grew wilder and she used a few cries I'd never heard before, but they didn't sound printable.

"All right, all right," I said, "I'll prove it to you." I got the tin-opener from the kitchen cupboard.

Slightly mollified, but still swearing under her breath, she supervised the opening of the tin. I wrenched the lid away and said, "Now, are you satisfied?"

She sniffed, but the scent conveyed nothing to her. She thrust her nose into the tin, then reared back, shaking her head, and sneezed violently.

"You see?" I said triumphantly. "I told you orange juice wouldn't interest you."

She came forward once more, still unwilling to believe it. Another sniff, and she sneezed directly into the tin this time.

"That's fine," I said. "That will improve the flavour no end. Thanks a lot."

She gave me a haughty look, sat down, and began to wash one paw meticulously. Really, it was nothing to do with her. And why I had insisted on opening that ridiculous tin with its uninteresting contents was beyond her.

"All right," I said. "All right, have it your way." I dug out an old briefcase and put the clipboard and the remaining tin of orange juice into it. On second thought, I added the tin-opener. I didn't know much about diabetes, but I knew that orange juice was a sort of emergency antidote to a coma. And if we needed that orange juice, we were going to need it in a hurry. There'd be no time for hunting for tin-openers then.

It was too bad that Perkins & Tate didn't run to a second tin-opener, but the clients came first. We'd have to rely on self-opening tins and jars for the next week or so. If the situation got sufficiently desperate, perhaps we might even resort to fresh vegetables and meat, as Penny was always telling us we should.

Meanwhile, I put the opened tin of orange juice into the refrigerator. Gerry would probably drink it later, and what the eye did not see, the heart did not grieve over. Not that Gerry worried particularly about germs, anyway.

CHAPTER

FIVE

SOMETIME DURING THE NIGHT, I HEARD THE FRONT DOOR OPEN and Gerry creep in. At least, I presumed it was Gerry—no self-respecting burglar would lower himself by raiding our premises. Pandora tensed and raised her head, but when no promising sounds came from the pantry cupboard, she muttered crossly, resettled herself, and went back to sleep. So did I.

The next time I awoke it was to consciousness of a gray, sleeting drizzle outside the window and a temperature several degrees colder than it had any right to be for this time of the year. It was going to be a great day to be stuck in a minibus with a tourful of unhappy Americans.

Pandora eschewed the day completely. She rolled aside limply as I got up, opened one eye, and burrowed under the bedclothes into the warm hollow I had left. She had the right idea. And her day didn't promise to be nearly so strenuous as mine.

There was no sign of Gerry in the office—apart from a heap of parking tickets on the desk. If he was planning to do the gentlemanly thing by paying that bird's parking fine, Perkins & Tate were going to have to find several high-paying clients. It would be cheaper for him to take up gambling—at least there might be a chance of winning occasionally.

I decided to breakfast at the hotel. I didn't feel up to the effort of cooking this morning. With luck, the members of Tour 79 would all have breakfasted already.

At least I had a peaceful half-hour, during which I finished bacon and eggs and most of the morning paper. Even when the chair opposite me scraped against the floor, I didn't look up, trusting to luck that, out of all the people staying at the hotel, it would not be someone from the tour. It was the last time I trusted to luck for a long time.

The table jiggled violently as knees collided with it, and coffee splashed into my saucer.

"Sorry," a voice said, "I didn't mean to disturb you." The tone told me that was a blatant lie.

"Quite all right," I lied myself. I bared my teeth at Young Horace. He showed his own—they looked longer and sharper than mine.

"Nice morning," he said. Perhaps he thought it was—for England. Tourists don't expect better weather. It takes them by surprise if they get it; if they don't, they simply concentrate on the cultural advantages they're presumably gaining and remind themselves that the sun is waiting for them back in "God's country."

"You should see one of our bad days," I told him.

He must have given his order as he came in. The waiter, with barely a tremour, set it down in front of him. He appeared to be breakfasting on a double portion of chocolate gateau and a large Coke.

Not to be outdone by a waiter, I concealed my own tremour. Besides, I could remember the winter mornings back in Cambridge when I set out for Harvard fortified by a bowl of beef stew and a wedge of apple pie. It's all in what you get accustomed to.

"I'm afraid I upset your mother yesterday," I said, to forestall him in case he had any idea of raising the issue with me. "I'm sorry, I had no idea of the circumstances—"

"Quite all right," he threw my own phrase back at me, and seemed to like the sound of it. He tried it again, clipping the accents a bit more. "Quite all right." If he worked on it, he might acquire the beginnings of what could pass for an English accent by the time he got back to his own territory. I wondered if that was what he had in mind in seeking me out. There were plenty of empty tables in the dining room.

He had something in mind, that was certain. He kept darting nervous glances at me. As though to reassure himself, he turned and glowered around the nearly deserted room, then leaned across the table.

"Listen," he said, "can I talk to you?"

"You already are," I pointed out. "I mean, go ahead." Instinctively, I braced myself.

"Like"—he edged forward a bit more—"you've been around. You're English. This is England. Tell me. Where's it at, man, where's it at?"

"At?" Even braced for anything, as I was, I reeled at that one. "It? At?" I was conscious that I sounded as though I were squeaking. I took a deep breath and tried to be more coherent. "What it? Where at?" It wasn't much of an improvement, sounding, as it did, vaguely like Middle English, but he seemed to grasp my meaning.

"The action, man! Where's the action?"

"Action?" And at this hour of the morning. I looked around nervously. Where was his mother? Why wasn't she here seeing that he ate a proper breakfast and kept his mind on the higher things in life?

"Yeah!" His eyes gleamed. "I want to slip the leash on those dodos and get where it's all happening. Like, where is it, man? Where's Carnaby Street?"

"Carnaby Street?" I went limp with relief. *That* was all he wanted to know—the way to Carnaby Street. Perhaps he wasn't so precocious, after all. I wondered if I should tell him how long ago the parade had passed Carnaby Street by, but I decided against it. If I did, he might want to know where it was happening *now*—and I wasn't sure I knew myself, it moved so fast. He'd be surrounded by enough American tourists snapping pictures of each other to be convinced that he was seeing Life in Swinging London.

"If I were you," I said, man-to-man, "I'd take a taxi there on a day like this."

"Good thinking, man." Elaborately leisurely, he stood. "I might do just that." The quick, telltale glance around the room gave him away. He wanted to get out of here before his mother arrived and stopped him.

"Have fun," I said, and watched him clear the dining room and the front lobby safely.

I began to feel cheered. One less in the minibus must mean a certain lightening of the atmosphere. It was a pity we couldn't lose a few more of them.

I paid my bill and wandered out into the lobby. Jim Davis was reading a newspaper. Kathryn Lamb was in the sedan chair making a telephone call. I thought she looked rather tense, but perhaps it was just the effect of shadows from the light outside.

It was ten o'clock and no one from the tour was in sight. That was the essence of Larkin's Luxury Tours, of course—leisure. There was no chivvying the clients about—no starting out at unearthly hours of the morning. It had been gently suggested to them that assembly in the lobby at ten A.M. would mean an early start. That was the Larkin method. When enough tourists were milling about in the lobby, checking their watches and grumbling, some of them would volunteer to go and chase the laggards themselves. Thus the tour was chivvied out more or less on time, while Larkin's didn't get the blame. If some of them hated each other by the end of the trip, well, it would have been the same on any tour, and they'd had an extra hour or so to sleep. Which was fairly luxurious, compared with what a lot of other tour companies offered.

Turning the page, Jim glanced up, saw me, and jerked his head. Obediently, I crossed over to him.

"Do me a favour today," he said. "Bag the seat behind me. And don't let them move you. I can't drive with someone breathing down my neck."

I grinned. "Having trouble?"

"She thinks my accent is 'cute.'" His shoulders writhed under some unhappy memory.

"Can't you tell her you're a happily married man?"

"I did, but she won't believe it. Her just having had her fourth divorce, herself. She says there's no such thing as a happy marriage. If you're happy, it just means you haven't found out all the truth yet."

I could see he'd had quite an afternoon yesterday. "All right," I said. "I'll try to get that seat."

"Don't *try*, mate," he said. "Bleedin' well *do* it."

"Cheer up," I said. "If I don't succeed, perhaps you can put in for danger money."

"Lot of good that'll do me when I'm—" He looked beyond me and groaned. "Oh, gawd, 'ere she comes."

I turned around slowly. Paula Drayton was bearing down on us determinedly. In her wake, not quite so determined, but still with some strangely disturbing resemblance to her mother, Donna drifted. She seemed to be looking for someone or something. Paula had found what she was looking for.

"*We're* here," she said, beaming at Jim, "and you're waiting for us. Isn't that nice?"

"You mean nobody else is around yet?" Donna's question was one Jim looked as though he'd rather answer. "Not anybody at all?"

"Am I late?" Tony Christopher hurried up to us. "I'm not keeping you waiting, am I?"

"*You're* not," Paula said pointedly. Donna glanced at him, then looked toward the lifts again. He was not the one she was waiting for. I had an inkling who that might be, but didn't say anything. Once would be enough to explain where he had taken off to.

"Oh, them again, huh?" Unlikely allied, their glance of mutual exasperation told me a lot about the way the tour was going.

This was confirmed when the schoolteachers hurried out of the lift. They, too, exchanged glances and slowed down, pausing to buy a newspaper at the desk before strolling over to join us.

"I guess we're not as late as we thought," Billie Mae said.

"We never are," Winnie said.

Marie Manzetti was next out of the lift. She, too, was in

no hurry after sighting our group. She nodded, rather gloomily, to the others, but didn't speak.

So the tour was neatly split into two factions: the college side and the others. A variation, perhaps, of the town-versus-gown situation; with which the gown, at least, was already familiar.

"I suppose we might as well sit down," Tony said.

"If you ask me," Paula said, "I think we ought to go without them. It would serve them right. They're always pulling this stunt. Who do they think they are?"

"Maybe they're in a state of shock, after what happened," Billie Mae said. The schoolteachers were in the middle in any town-and-gown controversy. It was neither their town nor their gown, but they obviously felt vaguely that they ought to be on the side of the education group, even though they couldn't wholeheartedly agree with them.

"Shock—hell!" Paula said bitterly. "The nosy old bitch got just what was coming to her!"

There was a nasty pause while we all digested this. Then Tony Christopher cut in abruptly, "That's no way to talk about a poor lady that committed suicide. You shouldn't speak ill of the dead."

"Oh, be honest," Paula snapped. "She was a drag all the way—always moping around, moaning about something, shoving her nose into everybody's business. The only trouble is that she didn't do it sooner—like, before she had time to ruin the trip for everybody else."

"She was an unhappy woman," Marie said. "Very unhappy. Be sorry for her."

It was smoothly, neatly, covered—but the implication was there. Again, I felt as though I'd stepped off a kerb I hadn't noticed.

Paula shrugged and turned away; the conversation was

over. Donna stayed where she was, facing the lifts, her face set in the half-defensive, half-defiant expression young people get when they feel their elders are behaving badly. Come to think of it, the lines of her face were already well set in that mold. With Paula for a mother, the expression must be habitual.

Kate emerged from the sedan chair phone booth and looked around, counting noses. She didn't miss the general restiveness, but Larkin policy forbade any direct action.

"Would you like a cup of coffee, while we wait for the others to come down?" she suggested.

Tony checked his watch. "Maybe I ought to go and try to get them? If we want to get started *today*, that is."

"Well . . . ," Kate hesitated gracefully.

"Right!" He wheeled on his heel and started for the lifts. Just as he reached them, one opened and the gown contingent moved out of it and across the lobby in a solid phalanx. I fought an impulse to retreat before them. There was something decidedly unsettling in the determined tread of their advance. Whatever was coming boded no good.

For once, Professor Tablor was in the rear—another little signal that indicated a stormy passage. Hortense Rogers marched across the lobby, the others trailing behind her. She, alone, appeared to have any enthusiasm for what was about to happen. She stopped short and faced Kate and myself challengingly.

"We've talked it over," she said. "We've been conferring for hours—and it's no good. We want to go home."

"You mean, break up the tour?" Paula Drayton snapped to attention. "You can't do that."

"Now, let's not be too hasty," Tris Tablor said. "As a matter of fact, we're not one hundred percent agreed on this step. This is just a sort of preliminary sounding out—"

"We voted." Hortense whirled on him. "The Board of Governors are all agreed"—she faced down John and Sandra Peters and Ben Varley until they gave small, unhappy nods—"that it is really the best step to take. We feel it only right that we should be home for poor Carrie's funeral on Thursday."

"Carrie was the last person in the world"—Tablor was still in there pitching—"who'd have wanted any fuss. She'd never have expected us to give up—"

"What about the rest of us?" Paula demanded. "What happens to our tour? It's supposed to last for two more weeks—Scotland, Wales, and Ireland we've got to do yet. Where does that leave us, if you quit and go home?"

"I'm sure," Hortense said smoothly, "that the tour can continue without us. If not, then I'm sure you'll be given your money back.

"By the way"—she turned on me—"I'm assuming that there will be some adjustment in the way of a refund for *us*. After you've transferred us from the ship to a plane, there should still be a substantial amount due to us."

It was just as well she hadn't made that comment to Kate Lamb. Kate, who was aware of the small profit margin Neil Larkin had to operate on during these first few years of getting started, had gone dead-white. Fortunately, my own face had no other colour to change to. My first year in PR had turned it permanently ashen.

"I'm sure we can come to a satisfactory arrangement," I said smoothly, neglecting to designate which side would be satisfied by it. "Meanwhile, now that we're all here, shouldn't we make a start? We're visiting Canterbury and the cathedral today."

"Following the trail of Chaucer's pilgrims," Kate said, coming back to life, automatically dropping into her monologue.

"We're not *all* here." Hortense looked around. "Horace promised he'd meet me downstairs. He isn't here yet. We must wait for him."

"Er . . . Horace has gone off on his own today," I told her reluctantly.

"Gone—where?"

"He . . . mentioned Carnaby Street," I admitted.

"Carnaby Street!" It was an agonized wail from Hortense, an envious one from Donna. There was no doubt about it, the place spelled Mecca to the American young and Gomorrah to their parents.

"*I* wanted to go to Carnaby Street," Donna said. "He promised he'd take me."

Both mothers immediately saw the bright side—it could have been a lot worse.

"Horace probably forgot," Hortense said quickly. "I'm sure he had a lot more than that to think about."

"You'll stay here," Paula said, "and go to Canterbury with us. It will do you a lot more good. And I must say it's going to be nice to get *one* side trip without that little wise guy making nasty cracks about everything."

"Horace is not overawed by history, just because it's old," Hortense said. "I brought him up to have a mind of his own—and I'm delighted to see him using it. Too much awe of the past indicates a complete lack of background."

"Is that so?" Paula snapped. "Maybe my ancestors didn't come over on the *Mayflower*—but I wouldn't believe yours did if you showed me their tickets. And furthermore—"

"Ladies, ladies—" I began, then caught Jim's glance and remembered what I had promised him. I nodded and followed him out to the minibus, bagging the seat behind him and putting my briefcase and camera on the place beside me.

"Shall we board the coach now?" Kate took up where I had left off and herded them out to the bus.

When they boarded, I was well settled-in, camera and flashbulbs spread all over the seat beside me, the picture of business.

Paula hesitated, then took the seat behind me. I could see Jim relax slightly.

For the most part, everyone took the positions they had had yesterday. I loaded the camera, stood up, and faced them cheerfully.

"All right, everybody," I said, "let's get a picture before we start. Everybody smile."

They hadn't much to smile about, but Americans are camera-trained. Teeth bared, with varying degrees of enthusiasm, up and down the aisle. There were the usual gasps from the unwary, who always look directly at the flashbulbs, and the minibus rolled off along the Pilgrim's Way.

CHAPTER SIX

DOWN THE OLD KENT ROAD, PAST THE OUTSKIRTS OF LONDON, through the Weald of Kent—and all in abstracted silence. No questions, no comments. Kate, who was obviously growing a bit desperate, was reduced to throwing a couple of expurgated Canterbury Tales into her talk. Even these brought no reaction. I began to miss Young Horace; even a snigger would have seemed more companionable than this.

True, they had a lot on their minds. Half the tour wanted to pick up their marbles and go home; the other half didn't. I could see both points of view. Saying so wouldn't make me popular with either side. The only thing to do was play it straight and let Neil sort it out. Presumably, he would have covered himself in some way, in case of absolute disaster. And if it could get much more disastrous than this, I didn't want to know about it.

We stopped for lunch at the usual Ye Olde. Under the thatched roof, some of the sharpest brains in the business had reduced the slivering of roast beef to a fine art. If it got much finer, it would be nonexistent. The tour apparently accepted it as a matter of course. All of them still seemed to be pretty much preoccupied with their own thoughts.

Mindful of my debacle yesterday, I got as far from the tour as possible. There was a small table in the corner, where I lighted with Jim. Even so, we were a bit too near the main group.

Kate had had to sit at the table with them, and occasionally, we heard her solitary voice, still trying to keep a semblance of conversation going. She was getting very little help. It was too bad I wasn't feeling noble enough to join her. At least, we could have talked to each other.

I was foolishly relaxing, rash enough to lift my head and look around the room. That was when my gaze rested on the doorway, just as Paula and Donna entered—they must have stopped off.

Paula met my eyes and immediately headed for us, ignoring the rest of the tour. Donna followed, as she always seemed fated to.

"There now." Without asking, Paula pulled out a chair and seated herself with us, and so did Donna. "Isn't this nicer?"

Nicer for whom? If my smile was a bit sickly, Paula didn't seem to notice it. Or perhaps she never got a wholehearted smile from anyone and was unequipped to assess the candlepower of what she was offered. At that, I did better than Jim. He stretched his lips in a valiant effort, but it was still more of a grimace than a smile. I didn't mind about Paula, but something in Donna's frozen wariness made me aware that she could spot nuances that her mother would never know existed. For her sake, I decided to make an effort.

"I'm afraid we've ordered," I said, handing Paula the menu, "but the waiter will be back—"

"Don't worry"—she passed the menu to Donna without a glance—"I'm on a special diet, anyway. Since I don't have to sit with the others, I'll have cottage cheese salad."

I tensed. Not another one with something wrong. What *was* this—the Invalids' Tour?

"I'm sorry," I said. "Er"—she didn't appear to have a spare pound on her frame—"is it a medical diet?"

"That's right," she said. "A doctor gave it to me. I have this weight problem, see, ever since my second husband. It's related to deep anxiety—"

Then it wasn't medical—just the usual American neurosis. I relaxed with cautious optimism. "Jolly good," I said, "then—"

She giggled. "You've got a cute accent, too. It's not the same as his"—she indicated Jim—"but it's cute. Where did you get such a cute accent?"

"It came with the throat," I said. "It was a matched set."

She giggled again, but Donna moved restlessly. Well, that good resolution hadn't lasted long. I took a deep breath and tried again. "Your accent is different, too, I notice. Not Southern, like the others. Not New York . . . ?"

"San Francisco." She rose to the bait immediately. "That is, originally. I live in La Jolla now—still California. I moved down there after my third divorce. After my first divorce, I lived for a while in Nevada, seeing as I was in Reno already."

"You've been around," I said, and instantly wished I'd phrased it better.

"You can say that again," she giggled. I ignored the

invitation. Once was enough, and Donna had given the impression of restraining a wince that time, too. Jim wasn't looking very happy, either, although he was obviously relieved that she had decided to concentrate on me, this time round.

The waiter took their orders. Donna, almost defiantly, ordered the American standby—steak and french fries. I could see the waiter waver, tempted to beat her down into admitting that what she wanted was chips, but something in the quiet desperation of her manner restrained him.

If I'd been feeling friendlier, I'd have tried to warn Paula about what the English called salads, but she'd put me off thoroughly—and the day was young, yet. Let her find out for herself—she was on a diet, anyway.

The one to worry about was Jim. From the way she was eyeing him, she had put him down on the menu for dessert. Well, he'd be nonfattening.

"You must like California," Jim said nervously. "You keep going back there, after living all those other places."

"California is better," she said. "It's a community-property state. You get a straight split, right down the middle, without any argument at all."

In the face of this recommendation, we both twitched slightly. "Me"—Jim wasn't going down without a struggle—"I think there's no place like England. It may be wet, and cold, and foggy, but I wouldn't live anywhere else in the world." As a warning shot across her bows, it was as good as any other, I suppose.

"You remind me"—her eyes narrowed—"of my first husband. Of course, he was a lot older than you—than me, too. But he was very set in his ways. He was a true gentleman, though. Even though we weren't living in a community-property state, he did all right by me. And he settled a very

nice trust fund on Donna, with both of us sharing the
interest during her minority. Of course, she was his only
child, he ought to. And I can tell you she comes into a very
tidy sum when she's twenty-five."

"At twenty-five," Donna said, her eyes narrowing and a
distant echo of Paula's rapacious look shadowing her face.
(Perhaps that was what had disturbed me about her. She was
too young to be so calculating. But look at her tutor.)

"It's twenty-five," Donna said stubbornly, "unless I—"

"At twenty-five!" her mother snapped. "There's plenty of
time. I'm not having you make the mistake I made. Although"
—her face softened—"I didn't do so bad when I chose him.
Not when I think of some of those other bums I married. I
tell you"—she leaned forward earnestly—"I sometimes think
I would be willing to marry that man again tomorrow.
But"—she leaned back—"he's married again, and she isn't
going to let him go."

The waiter brought our orders then. Lost in the dreams of
ruptured romance, Paula dealt with her limp lettuce leaves
and mound of cottage cheese without complaint. Afterward,
she retained her fork and speared chips from Donna's plate,
Jim's, and mine on an impartial rota basis. Occasionally, she
helped herself to a chunk of meat as well. She did it with
the same fine abstracted air Pandora used when doing the
same thing. It was impossible to say whether it was equally
calculated—she had seemed quite genuine about the diet.
Unless reminiscing about her ex-husbands had brought on
that weight problem again. I was briefly grateful that she
would be beyond range when the results began to manifest
themselves, if her problem had recurred. It was a by-product
Larkin's Luxury Tours hadn't bargained on. Some Americans
will sue at the drop of a hat, and Paula bore all the ear-
marks of one it wouldn't be safe to mishandle your chapeau

around. She was already too conversant with courts for comfort. She might decide she'd like a closer view of English justice, and given a susceptible chancellor, there was no telling how far she might go.

I resigned myself to a nightmare period of, for one reason or another, trying to keep track of everyone's caloric intake. This wouldn't be helped by the fact that calories had never worried me overmuch, and I had no idea what most dishes racked up. There must be a small briefcase-sized book about it somewhere—I'd better find it and keep it with me.

Donna waded into apple pie and ice cream for dessert, while her mother settled for an austere black coffee and assorted nibbles of rich, sweet crust. Some sort of distracting action seemed indicated.

"Would you like a cigarette?" I offered them to her.

"Aren't they tiny?" she accepted thanklessly. "I guess all English cigarettes are, huh?"

"All the cheaper ones," I agreed, discarding a remark about Americans waving around filter-tipped batons. The customer is always right, and in public relations, that goes for the customer's customer, too. At least she had put her fork down.

"They're not bad," she decided, inhaling heartily. Perhaps it hadn't been such a good idea, after all. I now had her full speculative attention, and it was a bit unnerving. I wondered if I reminded her of any of her ex-husbands.

At the main table, I saw Kate stand up abruptly. She had obviously abandoned the idea of trying to keep any table talk going and was determined to herd them back to the bus for the next stage of the tour. We were two hearts that beat as one on that subject—any move that would get me away from Paula was a good move. I stood up, too.

"I think we're going back to the bus," I announced.

"What's the hurry?" Paula grinned at Jim. "They can't leave without us, we've got the driver."

"Come *on.*" Donna pushed back her chair. "Let's us not be the ones to keep them waiting."

Rather surprisingly, Paula obeyed, but she fell into step beside me and seemed inclined to try to steer us toward the path that led down Memory Lane.

"Donna's just like her father," she said. "He hated to keep anybody waiting—he worried too much about other people's opinions. That sort of thing got very irritating. I mean, if he wants to worry on his own account, okay. But he wanted me to worry about the neighbors, too. Who could stand that? I was young and very high-spirited . . ."

I let it flow over me, heading grimly for the bus. Even during my sojourn in the States, I'd never really learned to stem the tide of sudden unwanted confidences Americans were apt to pour out. Now that I'd been back in England for so long, I was completely out of practice. I could only take as my guide that probably apocryphal story of the psychiatrists, one of whom said to the other, "It's getting me down. I don't see how you can stand up to it so well. How can you bear to sit there, day after day, and listen to people telling you all these terrible stories about their wretched lives?" And the other one said, "Who listens?"

Steadfastly not listening, I boarded the minibus and sprawled into my seat. Paula hesitated in the aisle, but I immediately put my camera on the empty seat beside me and frowning with concentration, began the delicate task of unloading and reloading it. She shrugged faintly and took her place in the seat behind me. I'd wasted about eight shots still remaining on that reel, but it was cheap at the price.

The bus was full, Kate said something to Jim, he pulled

the lever that shut the door, and we were on our way again. The peaceful English countryside rolled past us, yet there was no feeling of peace inside the bus. This, despite the silence. There was an uneasy atmosphere of too many people with too many unvoiced thoughts. Not that I gave a damn about hearing any of those thoughts, but I couldn't escape the idea that practically anyone's thoughts—except Paula's—might be worth hearing.

The low, sprawling, historic outskirts of Canterbury came into view. I was relieved to hear a murmur of appreciation ripple through the bus—at least they weren't lost to all the finer things in life.

"We'll leave the bus in this parking lot," Kate announced. "And we'll meet back here in about an hour. I'll take you to the cathedral—it's just a short walk—and then I'll have to leave you. They don't allow outside guides in the cathedral; one of the vergers will take you through and tell you the whole story himself."

I began to see the attraction that Canterbury had held for her. She was free of them for at least an hour. By the time they'd roamed through the town, as well, she'd have had a couple of hours to rest her throat and gather her resources for the homeward journey. She wasn't at all dumb, Neil's Kate.

Jim remained resolutely in his seat while they dismounted. I saw a glance pass between him and Kate and knew that they were going to slope off for a drink when she got rid of the tourists. Since I wasn't invited, I decided to go along with the tourists. Although I'd seen the cathedral before, I'd never joined one of the guided tours, and it wouldn't do me any harm. You never knew when a spot of historic culture might come in handy.

I hadn't gone more than a few steps when I found Paula

beside me again. Donna, I noticed, was lagging behind and
trying to strike up a conversation with Hortense Rogers. I
wondered whether she was genuinely interested in establishing
cordial relations with Horace's mother, or whether she was
just well trained to remove herself from the vicinity when
her own mother was on the prowl.

Or perhaps she was just bored with Paula's story of her
hard life—she must have heard the record many times
before. And I doubted that it improved with repeating. I
didn't even want to hear it the first time. The rest of the
tour, I noticed, were also well ahead of us and not turning
around to see if the laggards were coming. Evidently they,
too, had been regaled with the sordid saga.

". . . so, naturally, I sued for mental cruelty . . ." Not that
I was keeping score, but Paula seemed to have reached
Husband No. 3—an oaf with the nasty habit of expecting his
wife to get up and cook breakfast for him. A felony further
compounded by an absolute refusal to do the dishes or walk
the Pekinese. From the particular venom in her voice, I
gathered that he had not even had the consideration to
establish their residence in a community-property state. I
took a deep breath and tried to tune her out again.

We were approaching the door of the cathedral now, and
the others were huddled there waiting for us. Not of their
own accord, it was true, but because a firm-looking cleric
intended that the entire group should assemble before he
began his tour.

Kate's relief as she handed us over was an almost
palpable thing. There was a new spring in her step as she
walked away. I envied her. I already knew that I had not
chosen the better part—I should have spent those free hours
roaming around the town. I smiled weakly at the others as
we joined them.

As the tour moved off through the cathedral, Paula slowed her steps. It was pure reflex action that made me slow mine to keep pace with her. Before I knew it, the others were several feet ahead of us.

". . . but it was this last one that nearly killed me. That's why I'm on this tour now. It's a sort of convalescence . . ." To my horror, I realised that Paula was not going to stop talking. Intent on the unfolding vision of her private life, she might not have even noticed that we had entered a cathedral.

". . . There were times when I even worried about leaving him alone with Donna . . ."

The group ahead had stopped, and the tour huddled around their new guide, firmly disclaiming both Paula and myself. I tried to convey that I had nothing to do with her, really, I just happened to be walking here. Faint frowns appeared on several faces as we approached nearer. There was another verger hovering on the fringe of the group who didn't look too happy, either.

"I tell you," Paula continued, oblivious to everything, although she raised her voice automatically to meet the competition from the clerical guide, who also raised his voice firmly.

". . . St. Thomas à Becket—"

". . . that bum . . ."

"Here, at the foot of the altar, St. Thomas à Becket—"

". . . would lay anything that would go horizontal!"

When I opened my eyes, the verger was bearing down on us with the light of battle in his face. I tried to be philosophical—I had been thrown out of better places than this. Well, perhaps not better—but more exclusive. More expensive.

"Let's go." I took Paula's arm. "I need some air."

"That's a good idea." She seemed gratified at the response to her sad story. "It's dead in here."

I whisked her out of there one step ahead of the indignant verger, who pursued us as far as the doorway, then stood glaring after us as we escaped into the misty afternoon.

"This is a lot better." Paula twined herself around my arm and snuggled closer, oblivious to anything that had happened around her. "What do we do now?"

The wet mist was thickening—it would be a downpour any minute. There was one sure way of dampening any untoward ardour that might be developing. I smiled at her.

"Why don't we," I said craftily, "go for a nice little walk?"

CHAPTER

SEVEN

WE WERE THE LAST BACK TO THE BUS, PAULA LIMPING BEHIND me. There was silence as we boarded, and I thought at first that we'd been sent to Coventry, either for disgraceful conduct in the cathedral or for keeping them all waiting. But then something in the veiled desperation of Kate's expression, and the suppressed fury with which Jim gunned the motor, made me suspect that it was not entirely our fault. Now that I thought about it, there had been a curious quality of stillness about the bus as we approached it—as though Pygmalion's magic had been worked in reverse and the living people had been turned into marble statues, cold, unyielding, and forever silent.

The bus moved slowly through the late-afternoon traffic. Kate pointed out a few ancient buildings, but the ripple of interest these had stirred on the way down had obviously evaporated. Heads pivoted briefly in obedience to her direction, as though a switch had been pulled automating them, then swiveled back to stare unseeingly straight ahead, with no expression disturbing the alabaster faces.

She had definitely lost her audience—so completely that it seemed impossible that she had ever held it. And yet, there had been the beginnings of animation on the journey down to Canterbury. I wondered if anything had happened after Paula and I had left the cathedral. But what could have happened, in a cathedral, to upset them so much? To cause this complete and utter withdrawal into themselves?

Kate tried a little joke. It didn't fall flat—it just went unnoticed. At this rate, the homeward journey was going to be just great. It was as cheerful as a morgue in here.

And if *I* felt like that, what must the paying customers be feeling? They'd forked out a hefty sum for a luxury tour, and they weren't even enjoying it. This blank and utter silence couldn't be their idea of luxury. Silence wasn't *that* golden—not for Americans. Just in case any of them had had any lingering doubts about calling a halt to the remainder of the tour and demanding their money back, this ought to settle the point for them. Who'd want to travel under these conditions? Certainly not Americans.

"And so we say good-bye to beautiful Canterbury," Kate mimicked as the last of the outskirts gave way to rolling fields. No one smiled. I must remember to tell her that, although those old travelogues still showed up in screen programmes in England, no one in America had seen them for about twenty years. They didn't know what she was talking about. Or rather, they were taking what she said seriously. Just as they were taking everything seriously. Too seriously.

"I do hope," Kate continued, trying to force enough gaiety into her voice to elicit some response, "that you've all enjoyed your visit, and that you've been interested to see the real-life scene of *Murder in the Cathedral*."

She got a response, all right. An icy whiplash of repulsion snaked through the bus. The alabaster figures quivered and seemed on the point of shattering into tiny fragments, as though struck a fatal blow in the wrong place by the sculptor's hammer.

Kate felt it, but like me, she couldn't imagine what she had said. The bright smile wavered on her lips, then disappeared. She stared at them imploringly, but the faces were shuttered again. She surrendered.

"We'll return to London by the quickest route," she informed them coldly. "There isn't must of interest along the way. I'm sure you'd prefer me to be quiet now, so that you can digest your impressions." She sat down firmly, her back to them.

Which was fine for her. And perhaps for me. But were the customers getting their money's worth? From the look of them, their impressions were pretty indigestible.

It was a time for desperate measures. I took a deep breath and raised my voice:

> *From the tables down at Maury's,*
> *To the place where Loo-ey dwells,*
> *To the dear old Temple Bar we love so well—*

For a moment, I thought I'd cast the wrong die, then Tris Tablor's voice rose to join mine.

> *Sing the Whiffenpoofs assembled,*
> *With their glasses raised on high,*
> *And the magic of their singing casts its spell—*

One by one, the others joined in, irresistibly drawn by the power of the old college song, weak in the verse, but rising into the chorus:

> *We are poor little lambs,*
> *Who have lost our way,*
> *Baa, baa, baa.*
> *Little black sheep,*
> *Who have gone astray,*
> *Baa, baa, baa.*
> *Gentlemen songsters, off on a spree—*

Suddenly, I was more uneasy than ever. A new tonal quality had entered their voice. They sang with Salvationist fervour:

> *Doomed, from here to Eternity,*
> *Lord, have mercy on such as we—*

Kate turned her head, and I saw Jim glance upward into the driving mirror. So, they felt it, too.

As the last "baa" died away, the reflective silence engulfed them all again. Once more they were withdrawn, introspective, and—perhaps—fearful.

I thought I had lost the toss. Then, suddenly, Tony Christopher raised his head and began:

> *Cheer, cheer for old Notre Dame,*
> *Shout till the mountains send back her fame—*

One by one, the other voices joined in again. A little more hesitantly this time, not so sure of the words, but

willing. When the song ended, Ben Varley decided to strike
a blow for the home team:

> *Oooh, I'm a ramblin' wreck,*
> *From Georgia Tech,*
> *And a heck of an engineer—*

I began to relax. Anywhere, anytime, you can always get
a bunch of Americans going with the old college songs. I
sometimes think they could stop a barroom brawl in midfight.
They can rarely resist a singsong.

We would soon "Sail, Navy, Down the Field" and "Buckle
Down, Winsocki," stroll through "On Wisconsin," "Far
Above Cayuga's Waters," pay tribute to "The Yellow Rose
of Texas," and have a "Hot Time in the Old Town Tonight."

And if any of them had tumbled to the fact that I'd spent
some time at Harvard, we might even get a couple of
choruses of " 'Don't Send My Boy to Harvard,' the Dying
Mother Said."

We were all set for the homeward journey now, and
amazingly enough, everyone had snapped back into life.
They even seemed to be enjoying themselves. It was a
development I wouldn't have given you odds on ten minutes
ago. But it meant that I could relax—or, rather, settle down
to some concentrated brooding.

They were booked for a Medieval Banquet that evening (there
went Paula's diet again—travel is so broadening) and I had
a spot of bother trying to get away from them. They seemed
to feel that I was just what was needed at the banquet.
In case the management hadn't provided a court jester, I
suppose.

"No, honestly," I said, "I've got to go home and feed my cat."

"He means he wants to go out with his girl this evening," Tris Tablor said. "He doesn't want to hang around a bunch of old fogies day and night."

"Speak for yourself, Tris," Ben Varley said.

They laughed uproariously. Well, at least they were in a better mood than they had been.

I smiled and didn't contest the point. It was their holiday— if they got any fun out of imagining scandal about me, let them go ahead. They hadn't been having much fun otherwise on this tour. It would be a pity to disillusion them by letting them know how dull my life really was.

Back at the office, Pandora came to see me, complaining loudly. I could hear splashing from the bathroom, but the door was shut.

"Is that you, Doug?" Gerry shouted.

"Who are you expecting?" I shouted back. Pandora looked bitterly at the bathroom door and yowled an insult of her own.

"Don't speak to Pandora," Gerry called. "She's in disgrace. She scratched Daphne."

"She always did have good taste." I gathered up Pandora and went over to the kitchen cupboard. A clever, discerning cat deserves a reward. Pandora began purring as I opened the fridge door; a saucer of pilchards in tomato sauce was on the top shelf. She struggled from my arms, hitting the floor and bounding up with her forepaws on the top shelf, all in the same fluid motion.

"Wait a minute, wait a minute." I wasn't moving fast enough to suit her—no one ever did when food was involved— and she scrabbled for the lower shelf with her hind legs, keeping her eyes fixed on the saucer of pilchards. I caught her as she got a footing to begin climbing and lifted her away. She swore at me pungently.

Pandora in one hand, the saucer in the other, I crossed back to the desk that served us as a table in off-duty hours. It was probably encouraging a bad habit to feed Pandora on the desk, but she spent a lot of her time on it, anyway. You could hardly blame her; floors are draughty in these old houses.

I slumped into the desk chair and lit a cigarette, absently filching a pilchard from Pandora's saucer, just to nibble on. Equally absently, she gave me a halfhearted slap with her paw. Fish—all fish—in this place belonged to her, and she intended her proprietory rights to be maintained.

Just watching her relaxed me. The gleam of light and dark fur under the desk light, the way the bright blue eyes moved to meet mine in unexpected communication. For the first time in days, I felt a tight core of tension inside me begin to unwind.

Then the bathroom door opened and Gerry emerged, wrapping a terry-cloth robe—mine, I noticed—around him. Something in his attitude warned me that he had more on his conscience than simply nicking my prized bathrobe. I started to tighten up again. His opening words didn't help.

"Doug," he said hesitantly. "I don't know how you're going to take this, Doug—"

"Badly," I warned him. Gerry is a nice guy. A man couldn't ask for a better partner. A brighter one, perhaps. A less enthusiastic one, certainly. Even one without quite so much charm. But a better one—never.

However, when he started out like that, it boded ill. Usually, he was so ebulliently self-confident that it never occurred to him that I might not share whatever misbegotten enthusiasm he had developed this time. When it actually crossed his mind to have misgivings about my reaction, it meant that he had done something so spectacularly star-crossed that even he began to doubt my capacity for applauding it.

"What is it this time?" Tensed, I waited.

"Well, uh . . ." He ambled over to the desk and helped himself to one of Pandora's pilchards. Again, Pandora lashed out with her paw, this time with slightly more venom. After all, he had brought a noisy lady with a detestable high-pitched voice and unforgivable jangling bracelets into the flat to disturb her peace and quiet. And then had the effrontery to be annoyed with a self-respecting cat with sensitive eardrums for quite properly scratching her.

"Uh—Daphne wanted to know more about our business— naturally, I didn't tell her anything confidential. But she thought it sounded fascinating. I mean, she wanted to see us in action, as it were. She was awfully enthusiastic, and you know how she carries everyone along with her when she gets enthusiastic . . ."

She didn't carry me, but I nodded to encourage him. He was slowing down again and avoiding my eye. Which meant we were getting to the nub of the matter.

"And—uh—I'm afraid I've promised her—uh—that she can come along with us some day and watch us work." He darted a quick glance at me and added, in a rapid mumble, "Some day soon. This week, in fact."

Great! Fine and dandy! Daphne was all we needed this week. Dear little dizzy Daphne, with her dented white Lancia, taking a look at how the other half lives.

"She'll probably be disappointed," Gerry offered, as though that might propitiate me. "I'm afraid I might have made it sound a bit more exciting than it really is."

I could imagine. Public relations—one of the newest of

the glamour businesses. That gay, mad, colourful whirl on someone else's expense account. That never-ending merry-go-round where every grab brings down the brass ring—and sometimes, the solid gold one. That endless party with the jet set, the beautiful people, the—

It came with that blinding light that makes ideas seem brilliant. I should have suspected it immediately, but I'd had a wearying day. It seemed like the perfect way to avoid another day of the same.

Why didn't I let Gerry take the camera—and Daphne—and escort our little traveling morgue to Woburn Abbey in the morning? *That* ought to cure Daphne's illusions about the glamour of it all—permanently. With any luck, she might get so fed up she'd give Gerry the push. It would be the best thing in the world for him. And with his natural optimism, it wouldn't take him long to come to that conclusion himself.

True, I felt a bit guilty about Tour 79. On top of all their other troubles, Daphne was a bit much to inflict on them. Still, they had wanted to see English life. And the Daphnes were one facet of it. It might not take them long to recognise her type, and they might even find her an interesting study. Miss Richbitch—London style.

"If you're really serious about this," I said slowly to Gerry, "then why don't you take over in the morning?"

Pandora was enchanted to have me home all day. She sat, either on the desk or on the back of my neck most of the morning. On her periodic sentry marches through the other rooms of the flat, she would reappear in a doorway, checking, with sudden suspicion, that I was still there, and chirrup encouragement to me to stay there.

We had coffee and a saucer of milk for elevenses, and

shared scrambled eggs for lunch. During this, I got a singing harangue informing me that this was more like it. *This* was the sort of treatment a well-bred lady cat had a right to expect. Why wasn't it happening more often?

It made me feel guilty—as it was intended to. I'd known Pandora was a great one for company, but I hadn't realised how lonely she must get hanging around the flat when we were out. Come to think of it, I'd occasionally seen Siamese cats walking with their owners on leads. Looking quite happy about it. Perhaps it might be a good idea to get a lead for Pandora and she could accompany me sometimes.

The first tour pictures were back from the lab and I captioned them and wrote short, glowing press releases to accompany them. Penny had done her work well, and the list of local papers for each tour member was lying beside the envelope of glossies. Some of the towns had three or four newspapers, so I ticked the ones I was leading off with. There were more pictures on the way; there'd be coverage enough for all of them. Even if the tour broke up early, it wouldn't matter. It might even be a good thing if a couple of stories were printed after they'd arrived home. It might give them a pleasant glow, and this tour was bound to be one of those things that looked better in retrospect.

Penny, too, seemed quite pleased to find me there when she came in. "Oh, you're here!" She beamed, dumping a greasy parcel on the desktop.

Pandora stopped washing behind my ear and leaped down to investigate.

"We usually have a bit of fish and chips about now." Penny was rather apologetic. "I hope it's all right. I'm very careful about watching for bones before I give her any."

I took a mental bet as to who got the fish and who got the chips. I'd thought Penny was filling out a bit lately. "It's all right," I said. "But you shouldn't go spending your money on Pandora."

Both Pandora and Penny gave me injured looks. Pandora suggested sharply that I mind my own business. Penny was more polite.

"Oh, I don't mind, really. I like to." She stroked Pandora, who leaned into the caress, purring loudly. "She's such a nice, appreciative cat."

They were allied against me, and I know when I'm outnumbered and outclassed. I gave up. "Oh, all right, then," I said. "Just hurry up and have your tea—both of you. I'm afraid we've got some work to do."

"Ooh, good!" That was one of the things I liked about her. She was so enthusiastic. You'd have thought we were paying her enough to keep her happy and enthusiastic. Or even enough to keep her.

Still, things had been looking up at Perkins & Tate for a while now. If all the customers continued to be paying customers, and if we could avoid absolute disaster, perhaps it might be possible to put her salary up a bit.

If . . . Right now, Larkin's Luxury Tours was the stumbling block. They were operating on a narrow profit margin in this, their first year. If Tour 79 persisted in their intention to pack it in and demand their money back—well, there wouldn't be much money for anything else. Like paying the PR agency that hadn't kept Tour 79 happy enough.

"All right." Penny bundled up the greasy papers and pitched them into the wastebasket. "Are you ready to dictate?"

CHAPTER

EIGHT

GERRY DIVED THROUGH THE DOOR ABOUT SIX, TEARING OFF HIS tie and heading for the shower. Penny waved at him but didn't stop typing. We were going to get those overseas press releases, with their photos and covering letters, into the post tonight. She'd already rung to tell her mother that she'd be home late.

"How did it go?" I called to Gerry.

"Go? Go?" He halted and gave me a long, baleful glare. "Oh, it went well. Very well. Not a thing to worry about. I knew they were sitting there behind me—I could hear them breathing. It took a great load off my mind, I assure you. If it hadn't been for that, I'd have thought they were dead."

"One of them was," I reminded him.

"Poor creature—died of boredom, I expect. I thought for a while that I was going to. Thank God for Daphne—she livened things up a bit. At least with the kids. They moved down to the big seat at the back of the bus with her, and they really opened up. Couldn't hear what they were saying, of course, just mumbling and giggling. But it was nice to have sounds of life, at all. The others were fairly starchy all the way, but Daphne made a great hit with the kids."

"Fine," I said unenthusiastically. "Good for Daphne." She was, after all, closer to their ages than anyone they'd met on the entire tour. It gave me the beginnings of another idea—this time, not such a disastrous one.

"The others missed you, though," Gerry conceded. "They kept asking for you, if you were all right. They like you."

"Fine," I said again. They'd have liked anyone who helped them to keep their thoughts from the void—however briefly. They were also, I was sure, attached to Kate and Jim. They were—I became aware that Gerry was saying something else.

". . . and say hello." He seemed to be suggesting something. "It would cheer them up to see you again. Make them feel you haven't abandoned them."

"Down where?" I asked. "Cheer whom?"

"The tour," he said. "I just told you. They're downstairs—in the pub round the corner."

"What?" I was startled. "All of them?"

"That's right," he said. "They didn't have anything booked for tonight—they have a free evening. So, when I suggested that they come with me and have a drink in the pub near Daphne's, while I waited for Daphne to change, they thought it was a good idea. Now, they're waiting downstairs, having a drink with Daphne, while I change. But we'll have to leave them there because we've got tickets for an opening and they can't possibly get in with us—not so many. As a matter of fact . . ." He hesitated.

"As a matter of fact—*what?*"

"Well—uh—they seemed to be enjoying it so much—they've never been to a pub before—I—uh—I think I volunteered you to take them on a pub crawl tonight. If you're not doing anything else, I said. I left it open, so you can duck out. But they really liked the idea. It got more of a response out of them than anything else all day. Of course," he admitted, "that isn't saying much."

I knew what he meant. Presumably, they had had some enthusiasm for something once—for the tour, or they'd never have joined it—but they had lost all their enthusiasm along the way. And perhaps something else, as well.

"You know"—Gerry was still hesitating in the bathroom doorway—"it's funny. Considering that they don't take much joy in each other's company, you'd think they'd welcome a free evening to get away from each other and go separate ways. But they don't seem to want to. It's—it's silly, I know, but—it's almost as though they didn't want to let each other out of sight. I—don't feel right about leaving them by themselves."

"Don't worry," I said, "you won't be. I'll go down and take over." Of all the ways of entertaining them, a pub crawl would probably be the least painful. With luck, they might even drink themselves into some semblance of animation. If that happened, after all this time, it would be a pity to miss it.

"You will? Oh, good." Gerry disappeared into the bathroom. "Tell Daphne I'll be along in ten minutes—or fifteen."

Penny had been watching us eagerly, drinking in details of this latest scintillating episode of the glamour of it all. Actually, I was pleased to find her so interested; it fitted in with the idea I'd had.

"Leave the typing," I told her, "you can finish tomorrow—it's not that vital. Come along and join us for part of the pub crawl. There are a couple of kids your own age on the tour—you can have pineapple juice, or something, and sausage and mash on the expense account. Entertaining clients—they'll have more fun with someone who can talk to them in their own language."

She nearly tripped, rushing to get her coat, eyes alight. I decided it would be worth it, even if the kids hated her, to keep her happy. When you can't afford to pay a competitive salary, you've got to make up with little perks along the way. Amazingly enough, judging from the glow on her face, a pub crawl with a bunch of disgruntled Americans seemed to be her idea of a perk. I hoped she never grew blasé.

"Ar-rahr-row!" I was just opening the door when Pandora launched herself at me, with a war cry. She landed on my arm and climbed to my shoulder, berating me all the way. I was going off and leaving her again! Just when she'd thought she was making progress in training me.

She dug in on my shoulder, her claws grazing my skin through layers of cloth. I stood a good chance of losing my sleeve if I tried to dislodge her, but I couldn't—

"It ought to be all right to take her," Penny said. "She's very good, really. She never runs away . . ." She saw the way I was looking at her and blushed.

"I'm sorry," she said. "I was afraid you'd be mad. But I—I've taken Pandora out in the afternoon—lots. After I've finished my work. We go down to Embankment Gardens, where she can play. She rides on my shoulder until I tell her she can get down, and then she stays with me. She never runs away . . ."

I shrugged, bringing a loud complaint from Pandora, and gave up. There wasn't time to argue. I looked for the silver lining. If true, this meant we could save the expense of a collar and lead.

• • •

They were huddled in a corner of the saloon bar, while Gilbert & Sullivan selections reverberated around them, looking rather wary—almost timid—but more cheerful than they had yesterday. Of course, they'd had a drink at the pub near Daphne's and were downing another one here—that might have something to do with it. Americans are very fond of repeating the canard "An Englishman is born two drinks under par," but it seems to apply even more to themselves. However, I was all for it, if it would jolly up this party a bit.

They looked up and saw me. "Oh, look," someone shouted, "he's got a cat. He *has* got a cat!"

They surged forward, beaming, to engulf me. I had not callously abandoned them yesterday with a feeble witticism about feeding my cat, I *did* have a cat—and here it was. I was forgiven, applauded—we were all buddies again. It was no moment to ask myself whether I really wanted to be buddies with these characters—I was stuck with them.

I introduced Penny and channeled her over into the corner with Donna, Horace, and Daphne. The kids seemed pleased, but Daphne was inclined to be a bit toffee-nosed. I hoped she continued like that until Gerry showed up. If he found her being haughty to Penny, it would do more to break up that little affair than wrapping him around a lamppost in that white Lancia—which he would also take a dim view of.

Tris Tablor brought me over a pint and sat down beside me. "That, sir," he said, "is a mighty fine little animal, if you don't mind my saying so."

I didn't, and Pandora took an even more positive view. She stood, stretched, and dropped to the table, which she circled slowly, pausing to sniff at outstretched hands, with the air of an actress taking bows. Lapping up the admiration, she completed the circuit, stopping just short of me. She looked at Tris Tablor again and stepped off the table into his lap.

"Look at that!" He took it big. "And they say cats *know*. Cats really *know*." He was honoured, and he knew it. "Would she like something? A little drink, maybe?"

"Milk," I said firmly, wondering what he imagined Pandora knew. So far as I had ever been able to tell, she knew a soft touch when she saw one. "Just a little milk, that's all. And she doesn't need that. She's been eating all day."

A faintly wistful look spread over several faces, inspiring me to add, "You must be getting hungry yourselves. I know a pub just across the river that serves some of the best food in town—pub snack variety. We'll make that one of our stops, shall we?"

The wistful faces brightened. "You mean you're staying?" Paula asked hopefully. "We *are* going on a real English pub crawl?"

There was no doubt about it—at this moment in space and time, a pub crawl was their idea of genuine luxury. Something they could boast about back home. I thought of another stroke of exotic luxury for them. Neil might have a fit, but what the hell, he'd turned them loose for a free evening.

"That's right," I said. "And furthermore, we're going by London Transport. You'll see London tonight from the top of a double-decker bus!"

Out of the corner of my eye, I saw Gerry slip into the corner and claim Daphne. Donna and Horace hardly noticed. They were enthralled with Penny—she was closer to their age and more the down-to-earth sort of person they were accustomed to. They seemed to be hanging on her words, and Penny was expanding visibly under their attention. I'd been right—Penny was the perfect company for them. Perhaps I could arrange for her to stay with the tour for the remainder of their time in England. Even Hortense, I noticed, was relaxing now that the romantic duo had been safely turned into a three's-a-crowd.

"Come on, everyone," Tris Tablor roared out. "Come along! Douggie is taking us on a real, old-fashioned pub crawl!"

"That's right." As they gathered around us, I tossed Pandora onto my shoulder. "And we're starting right now. Forward, the Light Brigade!"

They took up the cry with a happy shout, and we surged out into the street, heading for the nearest bus stop.

I tried to point out the sights of interest to them as the bus rolled down Whitehall. Behind me, I could hear Penny keeping up a running commentary of her own. I glanced back; her two companions seemed to be finding it enthralling. Bits of their conversation drifted to me through the gaps in my own narrative.

"You people really get a chance to *live*, over here," Horace said. "Back home, they keep us in school until we're too old to care. Look at me, I'm eighteen—and I've got to go to college this fall, and that's four more years out of my life. And then, you can't get anywhere with just a BA these days, so I'll have to stay on for my master's. That's two more years. I'll be twenty-four before I can even start looking for a job. I'll be past it. All the best years of my life are going down the drain at school."

"That's awful," Penny sympathised. "It's ever so much more fun when you have a job, and earn your own money, and do all sorts of exciting things. Of course," she qualified, "I still go to school mornings—for shorthand and typing—

but that will be over in another year, and I can work full-time at Perkins and Tate."

She actually sounded happy about it, and I was relieved to know that she wasn't planning to leave us and get a better-paying job. At least, not in the immediate future.

Big Ben chimed obligingly as we passed, and that set off a great twittering and turning of heads. There was no doubt about it—Tour 79 was greatly improved by a few drinks. It was too bad that the luxury cruiser with its own cocktail cabinet was still tied up in Scotland with another tour. Perhaps we ought to change the morning coffee shop to a pub visit, beginning tomorrow.

Only the two lady teachers seemed unrelaxed, a certain tightness about the mouths suggesting that they had been in dispute recently. They were still speaking—but only jus.. Somewhere along the way, I must spend some time with them and try to get them into a more cheerful mood. If the whole tour could begin to enjoy themselves again, they might forget they wanted to cancel the remainder of the schedule.

". . . my blouse torn right off . . ." Penny's voice drifted to me and I had a sudden qualm. She was entertaining her guests *too* well. There was no need to spill out all the skeletons in the Perkins & Tate closet. I turned and tried to catch her eye to give her a warning frown, but she was intent on her audience.

And they were intent on her, gaping with jealous admiration. She had them in the palm of her hand, and she was glorying in it. Compared to them, trapped in their schools, she was a Woman of the World.

"But that was nothing," she went on, "to the time the tigers escaped . . ." I winced and tried not to hear any more. But there was a practised ring to the way she was telling her stories, and I realised she had told them before. To her schoolmates, obviously, and not her parents, or she wouldn't still be working for us. Parents are notoriously unenthusiastic about their offspring leading too adventurous a life.

Still, it was, in its way, enlightening. I had had no idea that Penny considered she was living the Rich Full Life at Perkins & Tate. All this time, I had been agonizing because we couldn't pay her as much as she deserved—let alone the danger money she was entitled to. It was slightly jarring to discover that it was the dangers that kept her happy and contented. It was also slightly jarring to realise that she had grown sophisticated enough to recognise their anecdotal value. She could dine out on them for the rest of her life—and she had obviously already started.

Nevertheless, I consoled myself with the thought that there was absolutely nothing that could happen to her on Tour 79. They were a group of fine, upstanding—not to say stuffy—American citizens. Discounting, of course, the raffish Paula. But there was no real harm in her, either.

Penny could safely accompany the tour for the next couple of days, keeping her own age group amused, and gaining some historical knowledge and a few luxury meals, courtesy of Larkin's Luxury Tours.

This was one Perkins & Tate assignment on which she would be perfectly safe. There was absolutely nothing to menace her here.

CHAPTER
NINE

FIRST, WE VISITED A PUB WITH A PIANO AND A COUPLE OF OLD music-hall turns appearing. That kept conversation to a minimum, which suited me—and none of the others complained, either.

Then, judging their mood, and with an eye on the clock, I took them to another pub before we went to the one with good food. A drink here, and then the pub with the snacks would just about use up my short list of quaint, atmospheric pubs. If I'd judged it right, we'd still be there when "Time" was called.

The party scattered as we got inside, several disappearing into the rest rooms, the remainder following me to the bar. Young Horace glanced around quickly and said, "I'll have a beer."

"You will not." His mother appeared behind him. "You're too young."

"I'm eighteen." He appealed to me, "That's old enough, isn't it?"

He was old enough in this country; I wasn't sure about his own. Licensing laws vary from state to state, and I think some states in the U.S. are still completely dry—a legacy from Prohibition.

"Why don't you have a cider, instead?" I evaded the issue, giving him a wink. His mother caught the suggestion, but not the wink.

"That's a fine idea," she said. "Horace, you have cider." To Americans, "cider" is the name of the nonalcoholic variety, and the other kind is known as "hard cider"—a fact that has caused a certain amount of bitterness in English people visiting the States in the autumn. Driving through the countryside during the apple harvest and seeing "cider" sold at roadside stands in gallon and half-gallon jugs, they rush to purchase it, thinking they're getting more of a bargain than it turns out to be.

"All right, cider." Puzzled by my wink, Horace surrendered.

"And I'll have sherry," Hortense said. "Bring it over to the table, like a good boy. I want to sit down."

When the cider arrived, Horace took a doubtful sip and a slow smile spread over his face. He winked back at me. "I think I'll get this for the girls, too," he said.

I was a bit dubious, but it wasn't up to me to cross one of Neil Larkin's customers. Penny wouldn't drink any more than she wanted to, I knew. And Donna could probably look after herself—with a mother like Paula, she'd have had to.

Having settled everyone with their drinks, I slipped out for a moment, myself. On the way back, I nearly tripped over Paula and Donna, just emerging from the ladies', and quarreling.

"Mother, don't, please don't." Donna seemed on the point

of tears and I dodged back around the bend in the corridor quickly. It sounded like a private problem, and one I wouldn't want to get involved in.

"You're too young to understand about security," Paula said sharply. "And you're all right, anyway. You'll never have to worry—"

"You can have it—you know you can. I don't care. Only please don't—"

There was a sharp crack, as of a hand connecting with a cheek. "Shut up and mind your own business!" Paula snapped. "I'll do as I please."

There was a momentary silence, which lengthened out. Not hearing any sobs, I eventually peeked tentatively around the corner, ready to retreat swiftly. But the corridor was empty.

"All right," Professor Tablor was saying when I got to the bar. "All right, *I'll* have an Angel's Kiss. You know how to make that, don't you? It's crème de cacao with thick cream floating on top. And I like it with *lots* of cream."

I glanced at him nervously. It didn't sound like a healthy drink for a diabetic to me. He was having a silent duel of wills with the barmaid, and as he was tapping the counter with a pound note, he won. She brought the liqueur glass over and slammed it down in front of him. The liquid sloshed about, blurring the fine dividing line between the liqueur and the cream.

"Thank you." Professor Tablor picked it up carefully, not mixing the liquids further, and carried it over to the table.

"Here you are." He set it down in front of Pandora. "Have one on me."

Pandora gave a happy chirrup and plunged her nose into the liqueur glass, lapping up the cream, pausing only to throw me a smug look. *Some* people knew how to treat a cat.

I ignored her. Since she was being looked after, I could devote a bit more attention to the rest of the party. They all appeared to be having a good time, more contented than I had yet seen them.

It occurred to me that I might chat up the noncollege group, with an eye to persuading them to remain and complete the tour, as originally planned. Half a tour was better than no tour—and half the refunds would be a good saving. I quite understood that the faculty and members of the Board of Governors felt an obligation to be home in time to pay their last respects, but there was no reason why everyone should leave.

Yet, when I joined Paula, Tony Christopher, and Marie Manzetti in their corner and delicately hinted at such a thing, the temperature immediately fell several degrees below freezing.

"Naw," Tony Christopher said. "Naw, we don't want to do that. What I figure—we all started out together, we all stay together. Right?"

The women murmured agreement. They didn't sound as wholehearted about it as they might have, but they were definite. It was as though some obscure loyalty had been forged amongst the tour when their tour companion had died.

Or perhaps they were just beginning to feel very peckish. It was time, in any case, to move along to the last pub, where they could sample some genuine English pub cooking and possibly, refuel themselves into a better mood.

Sure enough, with fresh drinks and tasty food, everyone's mood improved. Except for Pandora. She roved from person to person, accepting a taste here, a mouthful there, and grew progressively more furious with me.

She'd known—she'd simply *known*—that I was out living the high life when I wasn't in the office. And here was proof of it. Sausage and mash. Cheese. Cottage pie. Cream. Steak-and-kidney pud. Scotch eggs. Jellied eels. She glared at me with baleful fury. It would be a long time before I got out of the office without *her* again!

She was knocking back cottage pie with Winnie and Billie Mae when I decided I'd better make my peace with her. I ordered an Angel's Kiss and brought it over to their table. They still seemed to be at odds about something.

Pandora was just at odds with me, but the pie was moderately salty, and after a moody hesitation, she decided to accept my offering.

"She's cute." Billie Mae smiled at Pandora, nose-deep in cream. "He's nice, too. I still think we should tell him."

"Why?" It was suddenly apparent that Billie Mae had been throwing herself into the spirit of the pub crawl. "He's got a kind face and a nice cat. I think he ought to know."

"Billie Mae, you'll *hate* yourself in the morning. Remember Virgil?"

"Virgil was different." Billie Mae drew herself up with perilous dignity. "Virgil was a Rhodes Scholar."

Winnie mentioned a couple of other things Virgil also was. I managed to keep my eyebrows in place. One thing I had learned during my time in the States was that it was a multiracial, multilingual society. The most baby-faced doll prided herself on knowing the gutter language of several continents. Given provocation, she could tell a man where to go and what to do when he got there—and in his own language.

"Anyway, you should talk," Billie Mae said. "If you hadn't had that fight with Pete, and decided to teach him a lesson, we'd all be at the cottage at Lake Michigan, instead of—"

The party was getting rough. When ladies begin the sort of genteel blackmail that consists of veiled references to the past, it's time for a God-fearing gentleman to pick up his marbles and go home.

Except that my marbles—or rather, my cat—had crept into Billie Mae's arms and settled there, alternately licking cream from her chops and giving a sympathetic lick to Billie Mae's hands.

"I don't care." Billie Mae buried her face in Pandora's fur, then lifted her head and restated her position. "He's got a kind cat and a nice face. I'm going to tell him."

By this time, I had already decided that I didn't want to know. "Why don't we all have another drink first?" I tried to break for the bar, but an iron hand caught my wrist and pulled me back. There was no sign of a velvet glove.

"It wasn't—" Billie Mae leaned forward, eyes boring into mine intently. "It wasn't an accident! In Zurich."

"That's all right." I tried, nervously, to pry the iron fingers from my wrist. "I know. I understand. It was suicide. It's too bad, but these things happen."

"No." What bothered me was that it was Winnie who answered. "No, it wasn't suicide."

That left . . . that left . . . I tried one last, hopeless toss of the dice. "Natural causes?"

"No!" They both spoke at once.

That left . . .

"Murder," Billie Mae said.

I hadn't really wanted to know. I closed my eyes and tried to pretend that I hadn't heard that. My knees buckled slightly and I collapsed onto their bench.

"I thought you ought to know," Billie Mae said stubbornly.

"Thanks," I croaked weakly. If true, she had now made me an accessory after the fact by telling me.

Worse, they were both looking at me as though they expected me to *do* something about it. It crossed my mind that I never had got on well with schoolteachers. They had always found me inadequate to the demands made upon me, from parsing Latin sentences to keeping quiet in class. It looked as though I wasn't going to break my record this time.

"Are you sure?" I asked. I didn't really need their affirming nods. It explained so much: the curious atmosphere enveloping the tour; the reluctance to be parted from each other; and the lack of ease in each other's company.

Pandora wriggled free of Billie Mae's arms and went back to her drink. She was the only sensible one amongst us. Why couldn't the others concentrate on their pub crawl and leave their consciences behind them? And why choose me for their father confessor?

"But I thought the police in Switzerland were satisfied that it was an accident—or a suicide?"

"We lied to them." There was a sob in Winnie's voice. "All of us."

So, that made it conspiracy. And perjury. For a party of respectable, culture-seeking schoolteachers and citizens, these tourists had been racking up quite a score.

"But why . . . ?"

"We *had* to. If they knew, they'd have kept us there. Heaven knows how long. Until they'd solved the case. If they ever did. It might be weeks—months." Billie Mae groped for a handkerchief. "Years!"

I glanced nervously around at the others, hoping they wouldn't guess what I was being told. No one seemed to be paying any attention. Everyone still looked moderately cheerful.

Only Penny looked concerned. She was deep in conversation with Donna and Horace. Like me, she was mostly listening. Her expression was growing more worried by the minute. I wondered if the kids were confiding the same story to her.

"We *had* to—" Winnie said desperately. "We had to all stick together on the same story. Otherwise, we'd have been trapped—oh, my God! Don't you see?—trapped among foreigners!" It was as heartfelt a cry as any that might have come from one of her provincial counterparts in a similar situation.

There was no point in asking her what she thought I was. We were caught up in that good old Anglo-American Special Relationship again, honorary citizens of each other's country where, thank God, we spoke the same language. Sometimes, we even paid attention to the laws of those countries. But wogs begin at Calais, and there was no reason to pay any attention to *their* laws. Why, they didn't even speak English.

"She'd stopped taking those tranquilizers, and we all knew it," Winnie said. "She was so pleased about it. And if she'd taken any again, she'd never have eaten cheese—even though she loved it—she was really careful. And she *wasn't* suicidal. She was honestly looking forward to getting back to college again, and the exciting year that was coming up—"

"But she was careless with those tranquilizers, for all that," Billie Mae took up the testimony. "I mean, she left the bottle lying around on the top of her carryall. I kept telling her she'd lose it, but she said she didn't care. It didn't matter—she had her nerves licked now. She was only keeping the pills—just in case—when she got home—for the first few days—"

"The thing is"—Winnie was abruptly crisp and business-like, the schoolteacher explaining the solution of the problem to the backward pupil—"anyone could have taken some of those capsules and emptied the powder into her food or drink. She'd never notice—and everything tasted odd, cooked in that foreign way. She liked cheese and was looking forward to the Fondue Party. All anyone had to do was slip that stuff into her food, and wait. And"—the facade crumpled, tears were close—"someone *did*."

I tried not to let the implications swamp me. Someone on this cultural luxury tour had, with cold-blooded premeditation, introduced what amounted to poison into an innocent woman's food and then sat back and watched her eat the other ingredient that would produce a deadly chemical reaction.

And the other tour members, faced with the terror of unknown investigators and the danger of being detained indefinitely in a foreign country, had reacted with predictable insularity, closing ranks against the unknown law. Even though they also closed those ranks around an unknown murderer, it had seemed to them at the time the lesser evil. Only now, some of them were beginning to have afterthoughts.

"But why," I went on, fighting a desperate rearguard action, "tell me? When you wouldn't tell the police concerned, I mean?"

"Because you've got to *do* something," Billie Mae said urgently. "About Angie. Don't you see? She hasn't telephoned us—and she promised."

"I thought her name was Carrie . . ." I began, and remembrance slowly crept over me like a cold chill. There was one more tourist on Tour 79. One who had shared quarters with the defunct Carrie. One who had gone to visit relatives in Scotland, and was due to rejoin the tour for the final week.

"Angie promised she was going to call us from Edinburgh, to let us know how she was, and what she was going to do.

She wanted time to think things over. Nobody else knew she'd arranged to call us. But she hasn't. Why hasn't she? What's happened to her?"

I sat there quietly while they waited for an answer. Gradually, they both grew a bit calmer. They must have thought they were witnessing a prime example of genuine British sangfroid in the face of crisis and didn't want to be outdone by it.

Actually, I was too frozen with horror to move. I was also quite preoccupied with wondering whether my hair had just turned white. You heard of it happening over far less.

I have been here before. The feeling swept over me. And I hadn't liked it then, either. Carelessness with pills, and a missing American lady tourist. Yes, I had been here before, and the *vu* was *déjà*, indeed.

They were still watching me anxiously and I curved my lips in what I hoped was a reassuring smile. "I'll see to it," I said. "I'll start some enquiries in the morning—discreet enquiries," I added hurriedly.

They relaxed a little, which is more than I could say for myself. As soon as possible, I was going to get on the blower and dump this little problem back where it belonged—on Neil Larkin's shoulders. This was *his* tour, after all. And we would all be well rid of it, whenever it took flight for the States.

It had been a lousy idea to try to persuade them to stay on for the remainder of the tour. All I wanted now was to see the backs of them all. In fact, I was going to change tactics and urge them to go back. I'd do everything short of scrawling "Americans Go Home" across the pavement in front of their hotel. If matters got any worse, I might even do that. The day after tomorrow—their newly scheduled departure time—began to shine like a beacon for me. However much Neil was going to have to refund, however long Perkins & Tate had to wait for their bill to be settled, it was going to be cheap at the price.

The ladies were now going into the chapter and verse of their assorted fears for their colleague, but I'd stopped listening. I'd found a fresh and more immediate worry.

At the next table, Professor Tablor sat staring into space, a glazed look in his eyes, his face a strange pasty colour. Was he having an attack?

"Excuse me, ladies." I snatched up my ever-present briefcase, wondering if the orange juice would work on top of whatever else Tablor had been drinking, and hurried to him.

"Professor," I said. "Er . . . Tris. Are you all right?"

"I am fine, thank you, sir." He swiveled his head slowly to focus his gaze on me. "I am fine," he repeated ponderously. "But let me tell you, sir, without offense, that I would surely hate to see that little cat of yours trying to walk a straight line right now."

I followed his pointing finger. Pandora was weaving in and out amongst assorted ankles, looking more than slightly cross-eyed.

With sudden suspicion, I looked back at the table I had just left. The liqueur glass was empty and shining. While I had been absorbed in the revelations of the schoolteachers, Pandora had gone through the layer of cream and continued through the layer of crème de cacao, right to the bottom of the glass.

Pandora suddenly emitted a high-pitched drone, somewhere between a purr and a yodel. Meanwhile, she continued to rub against all available ankles and hands. One of them might be a murderer, they might all be conspirators, perjurers, and accessories after the fact, but they were her chums, her buddies, her pals. If she were able, she'd sing them a few choruses of "Sweet Adeline."

"I think it's time to call it a night," I said.

"I agree, sir, I agree," Tris said, still bemused. The others chimed in with their votes. They'd had a busy day, a better evening than they had expected, and it was nearly time for the pubs to close anyway.

"Let's go." I picked up my carousing cat and led the way to the exit. Pandora nestled on my shoulder, nuzzled my ear, hiccoughed a couple of times, and fell asleep. It was the best idea anyone had had all night. All I wanted was to get home and fall asleep myself.

But the night—the nightmare night—wasn't over yet.

We were at the top of the rickety wooden steps leading from the saloon bar to the street when Paula suddenly screamed and pitched forward. I tried to catch her, but it was too late.

She lay crumpled for a horrible moment at the foot of the steps. Then, as we rushed down to her, she moved, sitting up slowly. "Somebody tripped me," she announced balefully.

"No! Mother, no!" Donna was beside her, sobbing, reaching out for her.

Paula pushed her away and stood up slowly. One arm was hanging awkwardly, strangely twisted. "Don't any of you come near me," she snarled. "I don't trust any of you!"

You could hardly blame her for that. I moved to the front of the group and flagged down a passing taxi. "That arm looks pretty bad," I said. "We'd better get you to a doctor."

"That goes for you, too, buster," she snapped. "I'll find my own doctor. Come on, Donna."

"Well, that seems to be that," I said. Some of my sympathy evaporated as I watched her leap into the cab I had hailed and drive off. "We can't help her if she doesn't want our help."

"She'll be all right," Hortense Rogers sniffed. "Come here, Horace." (He had nearly leaped into the taxi with Donna, and this imminent defection had not gone unnoticed by his mother.)

Another taxi was cruising along, and there were hopeful stirrings from the tour. But I was in charge, and I was sick and tired of them all, and all their shabby little plots and evasions. There was someone far more important to take care of before I worried about them.

"Ladies first," I said pointedly, and squired Penny to the taxi, slipping some notes into her hand for the fare.

"Wait a minute"—she clung to my hand—"there's something you ought to know."

So they *had* been telling her. I was suddenly furious with them all, for despoiling innocence, for making a child another accessory after the fact.

"It's all right," I said. "I know. They told me, too. Just go home and get a good night's sleep. I'll see you in the morning."

"But—" She gazed at me in bewilderment. "But what are you going to *do* about it?"

"Damn all!" My patience suddenly snapped. I'd had enough of distressed women demanding that I take improbably heroic action. "Bloody damn all! Let them get on with it. Basically, it's nothing to do with us, is it?"

"You mean it's all right?" she said. "You don't care?"

"It's their business," I said. "Day after tomorrow and they'll all be out of our hair and back in the States. Let the American authorities sort it out—if they ever find out about it. You go home to bed and don't worry about it." I stepped back and slammed the cab door.

"There's just one thing." She was almost tearful. "They've invited me to go with them tomorrow."

"Fine," I said. In my wildest imaginings, I couldn't cast Donna or Horace as a murderer. She'd still be safe, keeping with them, they weren't dangerous. "Come ahead, if you want to. Skip school. You deserve a day out."

The taxi drove off as she was still trying to say something else. I waved cheerfully after her and turned back to Tour 79.

CHAPTER

TEN

I SPENT MOST OF A WAKEFUL NIGHT WRESTLING WITH MY CON-science and won a precarious victory. Tour 79 would be safely out of the country in another thirty-six hours. They were already beyond the jurisdiction of the country in which the crime had taken place.

If nothing else happened, there was no sense in my rocking the boat. I'd been told that particularly nasty little secret in confidence, and there was no reason to pass it on to anyone except Neil, who was my client. And he might possibly be able to do something about finding the missing lady.

The police might not approve of this view of the situation, but I wasn't concerned with their opinion. I'd always felt it was manifestly unfair that public relations representatives were not entitled to privileged communications, like priests and lawyers. After all, if PR reps started telling everything they knew, there'd be just as big a shambles as could be caused by a talkative priest or lawyer—and probably just as many candidates for jail and/or the divorce court. We were definitely entitled to maintain a discretionary silence. It was too bad the police wouldn't look at it that way, if they ever found out.

I had just fallen into an uneasy sleep when Pandora woke me, stamping on my chest and demanding breakfast. I opened my bleary eyes and looked into her clear blue ones. She blinked at me, bright-eyed and alert, obviously in far better shape to face the day than I was. It only went to prove that there was no justice.

"You made a fine exhibition of yourself last night, I must say," I accused.

"Prryeh-ow?" There was no doubt about it, she was not only unrepentant, she was quite pleased with herself.

"All right, all right, forget it." I struggled out of bed wearily, my mind wincing away from the complications the day held in store. No wonder Pandora was so carefree and unconcerned; she didn't understand the problems.

There was no sign of Gerry—I hadn't expected that there would be. I tried three times to get Neil Larkin on the telephone, but he wasn't around, either. Wherever he was, I knew that he'd turn up at his office at the stroke of nine. That meant that I had to start my day there, too, if I wanted to talk to him—and I did.

Pandora watched with narrowed, jealous eyes as I got ready to leave the flat. She stalked about, muttering sulkily to herself. I ignored her remarks but gave her a better breakfast than I bothered with for myself, and I continued setting new speed records for morning departures.

I thought I was getting away with it. I was actually closing the door behind me when she sprang. The door snapped shut, locking automatically. Pandora dug her claws into my shoulder (I wished tailors would bring back heavy shoulder pads) and settled down.

I was late. I was lumbered with briefcase, camera, and equipment. I'd have to set everything down, get out my key, and unlock the door. Worst of all would be the fight trying to get Pandora off my shoulder and back into the flat, and trying to keep her inside while I got out again. I decided I had enough in front of me today—I couldn't face that domestic drama, too.

"Fine," I surrendered bitterly. "Great. You're all this day is going to need."

"*Prryeh*," Pandora agreed, settling down happily. She thought so, too.

Wherever Neil had been, he hadn't been sleeping. I found it cheered me to see someone who looked worse than I felt. As usual, he was on the telephone; also as usual, he didn't seem to be having a satisfactory conversation. I waited patiently for him to hang up. What I had to tell him was really going to add to his misery.

Now that I thought of it, he looked strangely haggard— even for a nerve-wracked luxury tour operator trying to get his first year wound up smoothly, and running into more obstacles than he had imagined could exist. I suddenly wondered whether my news was going to be such a shock to him, after all.

"I thought you were going out with the tour today." He replaced the receiver and turned his long-suffering look on me. "Or is Gerry taking it again?"

"I'll grab a taxi and pick them up at their first stop." It could not have escaped his attention that I had the camera and equipment. "I wanted to talk to you first."

That information didn't seem to cheer him any. "You'll be lucky," he said, "their first stop is St. Albans—and you don't put *that* taxi ride on my expense account."

I decided to talk fast and get to the hotel before they started. "All right, this is your pigeon—you've got a missing tourist, do you realise that?"

"Missing?" He seemed relieved, and that did it.

"Apart from the one you had who was murdered, that is," I said nastily.

"Oh, my Lord!" The circles under his eyes deepened a good half-inch, even as I watched. "You know that?"

"So, you *do* know?"

"Know?" He braced himself for denial. "I don't *know* anything. The police were satisfied. It was just that Miss Carstairs happened to mention—" He broke off.

"And you didn't think it would be a good idea to whisper a hint of it to me? Just to clue me in as to *why* the tour was turning out to be such a disaster? Or even as a gesture of confidence?"

"I couldn't be sure," he said quickly. "She might just be hysterical. It's been a long season, and she's probably run-down and nervy and imagining things. Thank the Lord she had sense enough not to say anything to the police."

"But she confided in you?"

"Naturally." He drew himself up. "I'm her employer. Besides"—he deflated slowly—"she had to tell me why she was refusing to come back to England. She won't come back until Tour Seventy-nine has left. She's frightened to death of them."

We met each other's eyes and I could see that, annoyed though we both might be with each other, we were two hearts that beat as one. We were both now dedicated to getting Tour 79 out of our country and back to their own as fast as possible—and damn the economic consequences.

"So," I put it into words, just to make quite sure, "we do nothing."

"I feel it's *their* problem," he said. "It had nothing to do with Larkin's Luxury Tours. Don't worry, Carstairs is a smart girl—she'll keep her mouth shut."

"That's right," I said. "She doesn't want to be trapped in a foreign country as some kind of material witness, either."

He nodded, relieved that I had grasped the situation so quickly—and accepted it so philosophically. Then the pleasant expression congealed on his face as he remembered the beginning of the conversation. "What did you mean—earlier?" he demanded. "Who's missing?"

"A lady named Angie Hunt. She was supposed to be visiting relatives in Edinburgh, and she was going to call her friends on the tour and let them know how she was. They haven't heard from her, and they're worried. You might check the relatives—you ought to have their names in your next-of-kin column." I checked my watch and headed for the door. It was time to get started if I wanted to catch the tour before they disappeared down that Old Roman Road.

"Everything might be all right." I paused at the door and turned back to him. "On the other hand, Angie Hunt was sharing a room with the woman who was—who, er, died."

I closed the door gently on the vision of his ashen face.

They were just piling aboard the bus when I reached the hotel. I joined the end of the queue, nodding to Kate, who was checking us off as we boarded. She looked up from her clipboard and smiled faintly—the thought of getting rid of them all tomorrow was evidently keeping her going, too.

At the moment, all were present and accounted for. All we had started out with, anyway. Some in better condition than others.

Paula had bagged the seat behind Jim again. Her right forearm was in a vaguely lumpy plaster cast, which looked like the first attempt of some medical student making his debut in the Casualty Department. She'd discarded the hospital sling, and the arm and cast were suspended by a Gucci scarf that matched her costume. She smiled quite pleasantly at me and didn't seem to be in any pain, or even discomfort.

"Feeling better?" I asked.

"As good as you can feel with a broken arm," she said. "Still, it's not too bad. I've had worse breaks, skiing."

It was more philosophical than I would have expected of her. But, I counted my blessings, at least she wasn't threatening to sue anyone. Of course, she couldn't. Any brush with the law right now meant that the whole conspiracy was in danger of being brought into the open. Presumably, they weren't any more anxious to be trapped in England, while police, Interpol, or whatever concerned officialdom investigated, than they had been to remain trapped in Switzerland. It behooved her to keep silent and try to put the best possible face on it.

"Fine," I said heartily. "Keep your spirits up." The last was directed as much to Jim as Paula. Perhaps the cast would slow her down.

Penny was sitting with Donna in the seat immediately behind Paula. As I paused, Pandora dropped from my shoulder to the back of the seat and down into Penny's lap, yowling a pleased hello.

"It's Pandora," Sandra Peters cried from across the aisle. "Pandora's here!" Others took up the cry.

Pandora obligingly dropped to the floor and meandered up and down the aisle, greeting everyone with enthusiasm. She was in her glory, surrounded by admirers. That was a lot better, her triumphant glance told me, than being cooped up alone in the deserted office flat all day.

Penny, too, was trying to signal something to me urgently with her eyes, but Donna was talking to her and she was distracted. I winked reassuringly at her and continued down the aisle as the bus started up. Whatever Penny had to say, it couldn't be that urgent. We'd have a chance to talk at St. Albans.

Professor Tablor beckoned me to join him on the long seat at the back of the bus. He looked haggard and at a snap diagnosis, seemed in the throes of a monumental hangover. At least, clutching my briefcase nervously, I hoped it was only that.

The sudden doubt left me no option about joining him. If he was starting some sort of attack, the closer I was with the life-giving orange juice, the better.

"I don't want to worry you," he said slowly, giving me an immediate heart seizure, "but I'm afraid we have a little bit of trouble here."

The bones in my legs dissolved, and I slid down beside him in a jellied heap. "Oh, yes?" I still tried for the stiff upper lip—if only because it impressed Americans.

"I've been trying to decide whether I should tell you," he said, "but I thought you ought to know." He glanced around and lowered his voice. "Something's missing."

Why did people always think I ought to know? What had I ever done to give them the impression that I was thirsting for knowledge? How could I convince them that I would be perfectly happy to spend the rest of my life in blissful ignorance? More than happy—in fact, eager.

"Yes, yes," I said. "That's all right. We already know about her."

"Her?" He frowned. "You mean *it*."

I shrugged. "You know the lady better than I do."

"What are you talking about?" he stared at me in bewilderment.

"What," I hedged cagily, "are *you* talking about?"

"My manuscript," he said. "The one I started at the beginning of the trip. 'The Trials and Travails of Tour Seventy-nine.' It's missing. Disappeared."

"Disappeared," I echoed weakly.

"From my room," he said. "I thought it was missing yesterday, but I couldn't be absolutely sure without a thorough search, so I didn't say anything. Last night, however, I made a thorough search—and it is most definitely not there."

"I see." I didn't, but a glimmering was beginning to get through. "I take it this 'Trials—and—uh' is a record of the tour?"

"'The Trials and Travails of Tour Seventy-nine,'" he repeated firmly. "It's too bad"—he was momentarily wistful—"that we couldn't have been on an earlier tour. 'Tour Twenty-two,' now, would have been more euphonious."

Actually, if we were going numerically, he was closer to being on Tour 12, but it didn't seem like a good idea to tell him so. That's the sort of thing you can only admit when everything is going well. Tour 79 wasn't all that successful—and seemed to be still in the process of deteriorating. But that was the kind of thought I didn't want to admit, even to myself—what shreds of morale I had started out with were rapidly slipping away as people kept telling me all the little items they thought I ought to know.

"You're sure"—I tried to be helpful—"that you had it

with you when you left Switzerland? You didn't leave it behind there? You all packed in rather a hurry, you know."

"I am positive." He eyed me as he might eye a potentially trouble-making student, and I was suitably quelled. I was positive that he was positive. He wouldn't make a mistake over something like that.

"Did anyone know you were keeping this—er—record of the trip?" I asked.

"Everyone knew." For a moment he relaxed and smiled. "I can tell you, we'd been having a lot of fun with it. I've written up our adventures at the end of each day, and sometimes, in the morning, on the Continent, when the bus was taking us to our next stop, I'd read them out to the others—and it's brightened many an hour that might otherwise have been dull for us."

"I'll bet it has," I murmured. The conclusion was unmistakable. Somewhere along the way, he had observed too much—and written it down. So, the murderer had had to remove the notebook, with its damning evidence in black-and-white. The next question was: Would the murderer try to remove Professor Tablor before he remembered that evidence?

Tomorrow—I tried to cling to sanity and hope—tomorrow they would all be gone. Back to work out their dubious destinies in their own country. Surely, nothing would happen to Tablor while they were still abroad. The murderer wouldn't dare risk another death on Tour 79. The killer must depend on the semicriminal conspiracy that had already silenced his compatriots to keep them quiet and tractable for the remainder of the tour.

But—when they got back to their own country? Ought I to warn Tristan Tablor? Yet, he must be aware of the danger—he was in the conspiracy, too. And at this point, no one knew that *I* knew—except for Winnie and Billie Mae, who had told me. If Miss Carstairs, who knew them better than I did, thought it was too dangerous to come back to England while all these charming people were still touring it, who was I to decide it was safe to admit to them that I knew their little secret? No, Professor Tablor would just have to take his chances. He was old enough to take care of himself.

"... particularly unfortunate under the circumstances," he was going on.

"Circumstances?" I tried to catch up with him.

"Yes," he said. "Now, I don't know how much you know about the inner workings of American education ... ?"

That was an easy one to answer. "Practically nothing."

"Then I will tell you, sir." His face took on the set look of one mounting a hobby horse, and I braced myself accordingly. "The tragedy in American education today is the constant pressure upon educators to publish. It is no longer good enough to be a teacher. Performance in the classroom means nothing these days. What counts is the line of publications in the president's study—all written by members of his staff—so that he can impress the parents of prospective students, and the rich who are prospective donors of new buildings or ripe to endow scholarships. To prove they have a staff of live wires, who'll put the funds to good use ..."

He went on, but my attention was momentarily diverted by the view from the back window. Some maniac in a white car seemed bent on committing suicide, dodging in and out of the line of traffic behind us, taking appalling chances with oncoming lorries in order to gain a car's length.

"I tell you, sir"—Tablor's voice had risen—"the situation in which your professional educator is placed today is iniquitous. Iniquitous!"

"Terrible," I agreed. The white car just missed side-swiping a lorry. "Something should be done about it."

"Right you are!" he said. "And someday the authorities will come round to what they're losing by trying to yoke good classroom men to a damned printing press—forgive my language, sir."

"Quite understandable," I said, trying to pull my attention back to his problems.

"Meanwhile, there is no escape. It's a case of 'if you can't whip them, join them'—and I have been forced, literally forced, to join them. They have left me no alternative. I have an important paper coming out this fall—one that will be important enough to satisfy even them." He sighed deeply.

"Congratulations," I said uncertainly. He didn't seem all that pleased about it.

"It was too rushed," he said. "I should have had more time. Time to experiment, prove all my conclusions—oh, I know they'll all stand up, but I should have had time to prove them—"

"Everyone's in a hurry these days," I commiserated. "They'll understand."

"They shouldn't have to. Can't you see . . . ?" He broke off, shaking his head. The academic mind faced with the Philistine and wondering if there could ever be some common ground on which to meet in an uneasy truce.

"Nevertheless," he said, as though reminded of something, "that's why I must get my notebook of the journey back."

"You mean you had notes of your experiments in it?"

He looked at me sadly. I was the dense student who had failed the ten-minute quiz again. "No, no," he said. "I told you—it's 'The Trials and Travails of Tour Seventy-nine.'

Don't you see? It's another little publication—to follow up on the important one. Something light and pleasant, to prove I'm a real person as well as a professor of physics. It's also vital in the educational world today"—his eyes were as sad and mournful as those of an old bloodhound—"to show that you're a well-rounded individual."

And there were days when I thought I had it tough in public relations.

Come to think of it, I was just as glad I wasn't a driver today, either. The white car whiplashed in and out of traffic—it was close enough now for me to see the blond head behind the steering wheel. There was beginning to be something terribly familiar about it. But if I concentrated sternly on ignoring it, I might be able to spend a few last seconds in my fool's paradise.

There was a defiant, challenging blare from the horn of the white Lancia, and it swept past the bus to cut in sharply in front of us.

Jim stood on the brake, managing more by luck than by skill to avoid an actual collision; while those who hadn't noticed what was happening and braced themselves accordingly went flying.

"That's disgraceful!" Professor Tablor snapped. "Can't someone control that girl?"

CHAPTER ELEVEN

CONTROL DAPHNE? HER POOR OLD FATHER, THE BRIGADIER, would have laughed himself senseless if he could have heard that one. At any rate, I was relieved to notice that she was alone in the car. Gerry wasn't with her—not that he could control her, either.

Now that she was in the lead, Daphne dawdled along, looking back over her shoulder frequently and waving. Young Horace and Donna were standing up and waving back at her. The other tourists were picking themselves up and pulling themselves together; uncomplaining, but distinctly disapproving. Although this was the sort of behavior they might be accustomed to on a U.S. highway, it was not what they expected on a luxury tour of Quaint Olde Englande. Daphne was letting the side down.

Penny, looking a trifle tight-lipped, retrieved Pandora from the floor, where she had gone sprawling, and was trying to comfort her. There was no stiff-upper-lip nonsense about Pandora—in the middle of a quiet nap, she had wantonly been flung about and she intended the world to witness how badly she had been treated.

After about a mile, Daphne put out her hand and signaled Jim to pass. With visible relief, he did so. As he passed, Daphne waved at us, frantically mouthing something incomprehensible, and nodding her bright-yellow head like a demented dandelion.

I turned back to Tris Tablor, but suddenly sat frozen. We were just rolling along nicely when Daphne obviously had another brainstorm.

Again she applied the heel of her hand to horn and the heel of her foot to the accelerator. The white Lancia zoomed between our bus and an oncoming Jaguar—removing, I'd swear, the top layer of paint from each. With no room to spare, she sliced in front of us again.

I was vaguely aware that she had been trying to signal something to the kids again. But they, like everyone else in the bus, had been too mesmerised by the sight of that white chassis skimming the paint job on our vehicle—there couldn't have been a quarter-inch clearance—to pay attention to the driver.

Once more, Jim slammed on his brake, and this time, the dam burst. He was nearly as eloquent as Pandora—who had been hurled to the floor a second time and was carrying on like a Greek chorus invoking the vengeance of the gods—but a lot more comprehensible.

Fortunately, he was cursing in the vernacular. The tourists listened with pleased, academic interest. They knew they were hearing the real thing—they'd all seen enough English films and read enough modern English novels to recognise the words—but they weren't offended. Although

Americans are able to identify such language intellectually, it doesn't really touch them. All our "bloody's" and "bugger's" can never actually convey as much to them as one solid, rousing "Son of a bitch!"

It was obvious, however, that they were in complete agreement with him on his assessment of Daphne's character and antecedents. In fact, like me, they probably thought he was drawing it too mild, if anything.

"Open the door, Jim," Kate said quietly. "I'll go out and talk to her. She must want something—"

"I'll go—" Horace rose eagerly, but his mother pulled him down into his seat again.

"Don't you encourage her," Hortense said. "She's out of her mind—and a dangerous driver to boot."

"No, she isn't," Horace defended. "It's just—She promised to come with us for lunch in St. Albans. And she's late. I guess she's just trying to apologise."

"Well, she's picked one hell of a way of doing it," Paula snarled from across the aisle. "Trying to scatter us all over the highway is no way to say, 'Sorry I missed the bus.'"

"Naturally, the poor girl"—finding herself on the same side as Paula, Hortense abruptly switched sides—"was upset to find we'd left without her. One can understand her agitation. She is quite young, after all."

Paula drew a deep breath and seemed about to launch a scorching counterattack when, with a final wild signal, Daphne revved up the white Lancia and disappeared over the horizon.

"I think," Horace said thoughtfully, "she said she'll meet us at the ruins."

My first priority in St. Albans was a telephone. I wanted to check with Neil and find out if he had discovered the whereabouts of our missing tourist. Not that either of us cared whether she stayed missing or not—the danger was that her worried friends might dig in their heels and refuse to depart without her. (It would serve them right if we discovered she had picked up some totally unsuitable lorry driver and gone off for a brief idyll before rejoining the tour, looking as though butter wouldn't melt in her mouth. It wouldn't be the first time it had happened to a lady tourist on the loose.)

I hadn't many ambitions left, but the one I was cherishing at this point was waving good-bye to Tour 79 at Heathrow tomorrow morning. *All* of Tour 79.

I made my way to the front of the bus and crouched beside Kate. "What's the drill?" I asked.

"Morning coffee," she said promptly, "then the cathedral, the ruins, the museum, late lunch, and some time free for looking around the town and shopping. There are lots of good antique shops—"

"That will suit Paula right down to the ground." Tris Tablor had followed me to the front of the bus. "There's nothing she likes better than bargain-hunting. She's spent most of the tour looking for things cheaper than she can get them back home."

"I have *not!*" Paula refuted the charge as though it had involved something unmentionable. "I've hardly done any shopping at all."

"Oh, come now," Tris said. "Our bus waited for you all over Europe. We thought we'd lost you for good in that diamond factory near Amsterdam. Don't you remember? —when you got back you found some of us had been making bets?" He abruptly grew wistful. "I had it all written down in my journal of the trip—even you laughed when I read it out loud the next day."

Paula flushed. "I told you. I was looking for the ladies' and got lost. I didn't *mean* to keep everyone waiting."

"Yes," he said, "I thought I handled that very delicately. 'The call of nature'. . ."

The wrong person had been murdered, I decidedly arbitrarily. Whatever Carrie had done to become a victim must have been quite spectacular if it meant she had constituted herself a worse nuisance than Professor Tablor.

"While we're on the subject"—Professor Tablor turned and faced the others—"I have a grave announcement to make—"

"Stop the bus," I told Jim quickly. "Let me off here. I have several errands to do. I'll catch you up later."

Mercifully, he swung the bus in to an empty space at the kerb and I nipped off smartly. I knew what that announcement was going to be—and I had no wish to watch their faces as he told them, implying that one of them had stolen his precious manuscript. I did not want to be in any position to notice whether one of those faces changed abruptly, betraying its owner.

I knew too much for comfort already; I wished to know no more. They were strangers, one and all, with their own private problems and troubles. All I wanted was to keep it that way.

The less I knew, the less I could testify to. If it came to that. And there was a spine-chilling possibility that it might.

Tomorrow. Tomorrow. I clung to that thought, as to precarious sanity. Tomorrow, they'd all be skyborne and back to their own country before nightfall.

Godspeed the moment.

Neil wasn't in his office and Gerry wasn't in ours. Which was a pity. I'd wanted to find out if he realised his current bird was fluttering along Watling Street, upsetting the paying customers. Gerry has a very nice sense of the fitness of things—and that was the sort of thing that wouldn't fit very well with him.

I kept a wary eye out for the white Lancia as I walked toward the cathedral. I didn't want to cross any street that might have Daphne bowling down it. Come to that, I didn't feel too safe on the pavement, either, when she was around.

There was no sign of Daphne, and after a few moments, I was annoyed with myself for even bothering to think about her. Compared to the problems already besetting Tour 79, she was no trouble at all. Short of actually running one of them down, there was no way in which she could be a menace to them. Or to Perkins & Tate—so long as Gerry wasn't in the car with her when she went dicing with death along the motorways.

Yet, I still kept looking for her, with an obscure sense of unease. It was probably, I told myself, because she represented the familiar—almost pleasant—sort of difficulty I could deal with, if the need arose. Concentrating on her was a psychological device by which my subconscious intended to keep me from thinking about Tour 79 and the moral implications of their passage.

But why *was* Daphne hanging about the tour? None of them had struck me as so scintillating I couldn't tear myself away. I'd watch them go quite happily, and with a considerable sense of relief. Tomorrow.

The hill sloped down toward the cathedral and I recognised several familiar figures tarrying in front of shop windows, with Kate trying to urge them along, promising there'd be time for shops later. I slowed down. I wasn't anxious to catch them up, I just wanted to keep them in view.

At the turning, they took the high road for the cathedral,

and I took the low road for the lake and park leading to the Verulamium Museum.

Even there, there was no escape. Sitting on a bench facing the River Ver, I found John and Sandra Peters—and Pandora. They all greeted me.

"Come and sit down," John said. They moved over to make room for me.

"We thought we'd stay outside with Pandora," Sandra said. "It seemed a shame to leave her in the bus all day, but we were afraid people might think it was disrespectful if she went into the cathedral."

"That's right," John said. "Your little girl seemed kind of interested in the cathedral, so we told her we'd look after the cat while she went in."

"She's my secretary," I said defensively.

"That's right"—his brow wrinkled in perplexity—"that's what I said. Your little girl said she'd never been here before, and it seemed a shame for her to miss it, since she was really interested. It doesn't matter to us." He sighed heavily. "You see one cathedral, you've seen them all, far's I'm concerned."

"I agree," I said, a trifle too heartily. I'd thought he suspected Penny was my daughter, the way he'd phrased it. Not that she was *that* young—well, perhaps, just. But I was glad to have the misunderstanding cleared up, and a bit surprised at the vehemence of my reaction. "It's very kind of you to take Pandora."

"We don't mind," Sandra said. "One set of arches looks just like another to us—especially after all we've seen. Right now, the only arches I care about are my own—I think they're falling."

Pandora, settled in her lap, seemed perfectly happy and contented. I looked at her thoughtfully. Animals were popularly supposed to *know*, to be able to tell the good people from the bad, and react accordingly. Either the legend was wrong, or I'd drawn a dud cat. So far, Pandora had snuggled up to everyone on the tour, at one time or another, distributing her favours with fine impartiality and giving every sign of approving every member of the tour. If her judgement was anything to go by, the murderer must be Miss Carstairs, the courier who had remained in Switzerland. Somehow, I doubted this. It seemed more likely that Pandora was totally lacking in discernment.

As though suspecting that I was thinking about her, Pandora opened her eyes and gave me a long, enigmatic look. I returned it, and she yawned unconcernedly. It meant nothing to her that she was supposed to be a reliable barometer of good and evil. So long as people fed her, petted her, and admired her, they were all right in *her* book.

Still, she couldn't help it—I found myself making excuses for her—her formative weeks had been spent in a TV studio. What chance does a poor innocent kitten have of growing up with any set of values with a background like that?

"It's a nice day." John Peters pitched the stub of his cigar into the water and we watched a flock of ducks, swans, and assorted waterfowl converge hopefully on it.

"Too bad it's our last day in England," Sandra said. "After how long we saved to make this trip." The observation rolled out automatically, as though it had been delivered before—and often.

"Too bad," I agreed, and stopped at that. I didn't want to give them any encouragement about staying on.

"It isn't as though we even liked Carrie very much." The remark, although made to me, was directed at her husband.

"Respect is respect." His jaw set in a stubborn line.

"We could be respectful without going all the way back to

the funeral," she urged. "A nice wreath is respectful enough. Especially when the whole town knows what we thought of her. After the way she treated us!"

I didn't want to hear any more. A burning urge to see the museum swept over me and I stood up abruptly, collecting Pandora. Let them rehearse their motive for murder to each other, or to the swans fossicking for tidbits along the bank. To Pandora, even. But let them leave me out of it.

They stood up, loathe to let their audience escape. Once Americans have decided to confide their deepest and darkest secrets to you, you are going to hear them, regardless of your desire to. There is no way to stop them, short of providing an immediate and irresistible distraction.

"The museum," I said quickly. "If we go there now, we can be in and out before the others arrive."

They brightened and quickened their pace. If there's one thing a tourist can't resist, it's the opportunity to steal a march on other tourists. But it wasn't quite good enough.

"Carrie was a hard and unforgiving woman," Sandra said. (It seemed to be another, perhaps harsher version of Professor Tablor's evaluation of the late lamented as a "difficult woman.")

"I had the gravest doubts about coming on any tour Carrie was on," John said. "Only she'd seemed so subdued and different lately, I thought maybe it was time to let bygones be bygones."

"She hadn't changed, though," Sandra said. "She couldn't— she was set too much in the mold. Just like her grandparents and her parents. 'Right is right,' they always said, and so did Carrie. They were a very righteous family."

"Too bad the rest of the town couldn't live up to them." At the entrance to the museum, John halted and faced me. I was going to hear it now, and no escape.

"Once she thought she was right and somebody else was wrong," his wife said, "there was no letting up with her. It was disgraceful, the way she hounded that poor boy."

"Hounded?" That hadn't been the way I'd heard it, but probably the situation looked different to another woman. "The professor told me she'd defended him—against all sorts of charges."

"Oh." They glanced at each other. "*That* boy, yes. But not *our* boy."

"I'm sorry," I said. "I hadn't known—"

"No, you don't understand." Sandra was determined to explain it to me.

"Our own sons are grown up, married, and living in another state," John said, taking over again. "So, like most of the folks in the town, we have a student to board with us. Most of them stay the full four years—unless something happens—and you grow fond of them—"

"It isn't the money," Sandra put in earnestly. "Not in most cases—not in *our* case. It's having young ones around the house again. The noise and laughter and horseplay again. Your own student brings his friends in, and you feel a part of things. You make a lot of new young friends and"—she grew wistful—"as John says, you get very fond of them. Their joys are your joys, their problems—" She broke off and turned away.

"I think, Mother," John said, "it's time for us to take in another student again. We haven't been able to bring ourselves to have one for the past couple of years"—he looked at me—"because of what happened. But we've missed having young life around the place. We'll reregister with the Housing Committee when we get back."

"If you really want to." She turned to him with sudden

hope. "But"—her face darkened—"if we do that—right on top of Carrie's dying, won't people think . . . ?"

"They wouldn't expect us to be chief mourners, anyhow." Again, the gaunt face tightened. "Not after what Carrie did."

"What *did* she do?" I couldn't stop myself asking. I didn't want to be involved, but my momentary curiosity outstripped my natural cowardice.

"We had a fine young man staying with us a couple of years ago. He came to us in his freshman year—and I swear to you he was as fine and upstanding a young fellow as I've ever seen. Just high-spirited, that was all—"

"I see." I'd heard that one before. Probably I'd heard it all before, but I was committed to hearing it again now.

"We never had any trouble with him. The authorities never had any trouble with him. There was none of that nonsense about marching around, demonstrating, or"—his mouth twisted bitterly—"drugs."

I began to see where this might be leading. Sure enough—

"Then, in his junior year, he ran afoul of Carrie's pet drug addict. No, he didn't start experimenting with drugs—" He held up his hand, cutting off the idea before it had time to form fully in my mind. "He was too sensible for that. They played cards together, that was all. For money. Oh, perhaps he shouldn't have, I agree—"

"There was nothing wrong in it," Sandra defended immediately. "He'd have paid, if he'd lost. But naturally, with that other one in the state he was usually in—"

"I take it,' I said, "that your—er—boy won. Won . . . heavily, perhaps?"

"No 'perhaps' about it," John said with proprietary pride. "He took that lousy drug-taker to the cleaners. And why not? He could afford it. You look at someone like that, given every advantage, no need to struggle . . ."

Perhaps that was the trouble. But I said it silently. It was obvious that we were reaching the core of the American dilemma, and a sore and tender core it was. It was not for me to offer facile comments.

"The best of everything, good home, fine parents, plenty of spending money, and—"

"And everyone falling all over themselves every time he opened his mouth," Sandra finished bitterly. "Especially Carrie. If he was so smart, what was he doing drugging himself like that? 'A great career in front of him'—like fun! He landed up just where everybody knows those kind land up—swinging from a shower rail, on one of his trips."

"Now, now, Mother." John tried to calm her, but it was apparent that the conversation had struck a throbbing nerve.

"Carrie shouldn't have done it," she wailed. "She shouldn't have. Accusing that poor, dear boy of cheating. Just because her tame drug addict was too far gone to see the cards he was holding, let alone play them. It was wicked of Carrie—wicked! And God punished her!"

"Sandra!" John thundered. He glanced at me nervously. "I'm sorry. Mother still gets a mite het up about it. Not that I blame her. Carrie just wasn't normal about that boy. But you can't condemn her entirely. It was partly her age, and partly her position in the community, and—"

"Quite," I said hastily. We were getting into deep, unchartered waters here. "Quite."

"It was a lie," Sandra said firmly. "A wicked lie. And Carrie kept repeating it. Everyone knows if you fling enough mud, some of it will stick. And Carrie made it stick. She saw to it that Bert was expelled. Much good it did her," she added vindictively. "It didn't save her 'brilliant' drugger, and—in the end—it didn't save *her*, either."

"Mother!" Her husband grabbed her by the shoulders and shook her sharply. She took a couple of deep, shuddering breaths and seemed to regain control.

"I don't care," she said stubbornly. "Carrie deserved everything that happened to her—and that's the truth."

"We're here in England now." Again her husband called her back to reality. "That's over. A long time ago. We might as well go in and look at this museum, as long as we're here."

They seemed to have forgotten me, for which I was grateful. I watched them walk slowly into the museum, two elderly people, arm in arm, who had slipped into the trap of trying to live their lives through a younger generation. Who had taken on the joys and sorrows of someone else, and found themselves close to heartbreak through the machinations of a harsh, unforgiving, relentless woman. Who had hated that woman for the sake of their protégé.

Enough to murder her?

CHAPTER
TWELVE

I LOOKED UP TO SEE PENNY BEARING DOWN ON ME. SHE HAD
the look in her eye of a woman determined to tell me something unpleasant. For my own good, of course. That decided
me. It was six of one and half-dozen of the other—and I'd
already been hit for six by the two inside the museum.
There was nothing else that they could do to me. Especially
if I managed to keep my distance.

"Here." As Penny approached, I held Pandora out to her.
"Take care of Pandora while I look through the museum.
Then I'll take her while you go through. We might as well
see the place, now that we're here."

Sandra and John were well ahead of me, looking blankly
as the display cases on the far wall. Just a couple of
pleasant, elderly American tourists again, doing their duty
by grimly amassing all the culture on offer, absorbing
history until it threatened to run out of their ears, and seeming

a bit dazed by it all. They'd be much happier when they got back home and could project their slides onto a screen and relive it all in the comfort of their home, while boring the neighbours to tears.

I sauntered slowly around the museum, keeping well behind them. It was a nice little museum, as museums go. So far as I'm concerned, there's always too much emphasis on the dead in the dead past, and I wondered what the tourists would think as they were paraded past the artifacts of one more dead civilization. The assortment of skeletons was too graphic a reminder of our inevitable end at the best of times. And this was not the best of times for Tour 79; the spirit of the relentless Carrie seemed always to be with them, a ghost unwilling to be laid to rest by time and distance. Some of them—one of them—must be made very pensive at the sight of the crumbling skeleton in the lead coffin.

It was well that the museum was scheduled before lunch. Mere loss of appetite wasn't so drastic as an attack of conscience on a full stomach might be.

I heard a commotion at the entrance, which meant that the rest of the tour had caught up with us. That was my cue to slide out quietly. I didn't want to watch them going around the exhibits. I might catch more expression than intended on one of the faces, and I didn't want to know.

Nodding pleasantly to them as I passed, I went back outside. After a minute, I found Penny around at the back, sitting on a stone and gazing thoughtfully into the middle distance, utterly oblivious to everything around her. She was alone.

"Where's Pandora?" I asked.

"Pandora?" She looked around vaguely. "She won't go

far. She's very good about that. Look, I think you ought to know—"

"Later." I had spotted Pandora. With impractical ambition, she was stalking a large white swan. (Perhaps it was time I fed her.) I raced down the bank and caught her just as she was crouching to spring.

"Pick on something your own size." I snatched her up, ignoring her bitter complaints. I was always spoiling her fun.

Penny was standing up, frowning, when I returned. "You'd better hurry," I told her. "The others are already going through the museum. It won't take them long—they looked ready for lunch. If you don't hurry, you'll miss it."

"Yes," she said, but still seemed reluctant to move away. "Yes, but honestly, I think I ought to tell you—"

"I know all about it," I assured her. "Believe me, the situation is well in hand—or as in hand as it can get. The thing to do is just hold tight and concentrate on tomorrow. They'll all be gone then. Meanwhile, don't worry about it."

"Well"—she still seemed dubious—"if you're sure."

"I'm positive," I said rashly. "Just run along and we'll see you at lunch."

It was all going smoothly now. With the end in sight, I could begin to relax. I strolled down into the village and into the nearest pub. Pubs have telephones, along with their other attractive features, and I still hadn't managed to contact Neil.

Pandora twitched restlessly on my shoulder. She knew all about pubs, too. They had sausages, cheese, and other delicious items—plus a lot of friendly people ever willing to share a snack with a hungry cat. Why were we wasting time in this phone booth?

It was a good question. Neil wasn't available. Gerry still

appeared to be elsewhere than the office. However, through the glass, I could see Jim signaling me to come and join him when I finished telephoning. He looked as though he needed cheering.

"What-ho!" I greeted him, and gave my order to the barmaid.

"What-bloody-ho, yourself," he said glumly. "Same again."

I looked at him closely and the alarm bells started ringing wildly. That wasn't going to be his second drink, perhaps not even his third. And he was driving. What kind of PR can you do for a tourist company with a driver in jail for drunken driving? It didn't bear thinking about. I had to say something.

"Er," I said carefully, "do you really think you ought?"

"Yes, I ought." He didn't try to pretend that he didn't know what I was talking about. "Don't worry, mate, it's dead easy. If they stop you with that breathalyser, you say you've been eating pickled onions. And I 'ave, too, see?"

There was a plate of cheese and pickled onions in front of him. Pandora dropped from my shoulder to the bar and approached the plate cautiously, with a hopeful look.

"'Ere you are, mate." He rolled a small pickled onion over to her. "'Ave one one me."

Pandora sniffed at it delicately, recoiled, and tried to bury it. She had the right idea.

"No gratitude," Jim said gloomily. "That's the trouble with the whole bloody world. No gratitude and no sense."

"Here." I reached around the heated showcase and took a sausage, breaking it into manageable bits, and gave some to Pandora. She was mollified instantly. That was more than I could do for Jim.

"Take me," he said. "If I had sense, would I be here? No," he answered himself. "There I was—sitting pretty. I drove a bus for London Transport. All shut away, safelike, from the bleedin' passengers. But did I appreciate it? No."

He was doing fine, asking and answering the questions himself. I leaned back and let him get on with it.

"No, I wanted more money, I wanted to drive someplace besides London. I was so bloody daft I even thought it would be nice to meet the passengers and get a chance to chat them up. *Gaarh!*"

"It hasn't been so bad, has it?" I really wanted to know. "Before this particular tour group, I mean?"

"One like this is all you need to put you on the turn," he said. "I thought that dirty great plaster cast might slow her down, but it hasn't. Not a bit. Do you know what she did this morning? Gawdstrewth—she pinched me!" He brooded into his drink.

"Tomorrow." It was the one rallying cry I had to cheer the troups with. "Tomorrow they'll be gone. Concentrate on that. Two more drives. Back to London this afternoon, and then out to Heathrow in the morning, and we're free of them. They'll all go back where they came from, and you can relax."

"Relax?" He was bitter. "And 'ow about that drive back to London? I mean, 'ow about that blond bint wiv the car? I don't go a bundle on playing 'Chase-me-Charlie' down Watling Street wiv *that* nutter again."

He had an excellent point there. I wasn't too anxious to be in any bus that Daphne was playing tag with, either. I'd rather have Jim driving drunk than Daphne sober.

"I'll try to speak to her," I said. One word from me and she'd do as she pleased, but I hoped I sounded authoritative enough to put Jim's mind at rest. Meanwhile, it might be a good idea to get some food into him. Cheese and pickled onions might be tasty, but I doubted their effectiveness as blotting paper.

"Let's go and join the others for lunch," I suggested. "Do you know where we're eating?"

"Hotel up the road and around the corner." He gestured. "You go. I'll stop 'ere."

That was just what I was trying to avoid. It took me some time, but I managed to persuade him to accompany me.

Lunch was leisurely and uneventful. There was a certain amount of discussion about the sights already covered. Mostly, they were looking forward to the remainder of the day. With delicate regard for aching feet, the afternoon schedule after shopping called for a "Ride Through Rural England," afternoon tea, and "Return to London." After a solid morning through cathedral, ruins, and museum, this was just about everyone's speed. Including mine. As someone has noted somewhere before, culture is very hard on the feet. I had to admire Neil's grasp of psychology.

I admired it even more later that afternoon when I saw the tearoom. It was so Olde Worlde it was like dining in a display case in a museum. I wondered if he'd had it built to order. The actual tea, however, was well above standard for such places and the service was excellent.

There was even a telephone. Neil was still among the missing, but I managed to get hold of Gerry this time. He was in a better mood than I was, but I soon fixed that.

"No, I don't know where Daphne is," he said, a bit warily. "Why should I know? I'm meeting her for dinner tonight. Other than that, what she does all day is her business. I've been working—I think we've landed a new account. It's—"

"Daphne's here," I told him. There was time to hear the

rest later. "Daphne appears to have joined the tour—adopted it, in fact. She's been dogging our footsteps all day, and if she doesn't give some of them a heart attack with her driving, we'll be lucky."

"There? What's she doing there?"

"I just told you. She's giving the customers a collective nervous breakdown, playing motorway leapfrog with our bus."

"She's doing that?" I could sense Gerry's shudder. "Daphne is mucking up our meal tickets?" He seemed to find it hard to believe that she had put herself so far beyond the pale. He always did take the kindest view of everyone. Obviously, he had never looked at Daphne closely—and seldom in daylight.

"She is tearing them into tiny, nerve-wracked shreds," I assured him. "Which is nothing to what she's doing to our driver, who's had to try to dodge her."

"But—that's serious," Gerry said incredulously. "Daphne shouldn't be doing that."

"Precisely." Agreed at last. "But she is."

"Is she there? Call her to the telephone. Let me talk to her for a minute." He sounded as though he really thought he could persuade her into being reasonable. Still, it was worth a try.

I turned from the phone just in time to see a flash of yellow at eye level as Daphne dashed past, followed by Donna and Horace. I called to her, wrenching the door open, and collided with Penny, who was also moving in that direction.

"Here"—Penny thrust Pandora into my arms—"I'm going with them." She glared at me accusingly. "You said everything was under control!"

"It is," I said. "My God—isn't it?" Something in her attitude set the alarm bells jangling again.

"Oh, I might have known you were too calm," she wailed.

"What's the matter? Tell me!" Outside, the motor of the white Lancia revved up wildly.

"I can't stop," Penny said. "Telephone my mother, that's all. Just telephone my mother."

"Why? What should I tell her?" But she was already dashing away.

"Telephone her," her voice came floating back to me, "when you find out what it's all about."

I hung up on Gerry quickly, barely registering his promise to meet us at the hotel and deal with Daphne severely. In Gerry's vocabulary, this simply meant taking her to a cheaper restaurant as a sign of disapproval. Gerry is so subtle that some of his birds have been on his blacklist for months and never realised it until they found themselves walking down the aisle on the arm of some old school chum he'd introduced them to. At such moments, you could see a faint puzzled light in their eyes, as though they wondered how the groom they'd planned on had been switched at the last minute.

Hoisting Pandora to my shoulder, I rejoined the others cautiously. To my relief, nothing untoward seemed to have taken place. They were all filing out to the bus again and appeared quite pleased with their tea. If there was any disaster I had to telephone and report to Penny's mother, I couldn't see what it was.

"Have I missed anything?" They looked at me oddly. "I mean, I saw Daphne and the kids go tearing past. I thought perhaps—" I paused, hoping I wasn't going to have to finish that sentence.

"They've gone ahead." Fortunately, Hortense answered. "My Horace is going to drive for a while, to keep that girl from trying to kill herself, and us with her. The girls have gone along to keep them company. With all of them in the car, they can persuade her not to drive so fast. It was Horace's idea," she added smugly. "He's very clever."

Jim was looking a great deal more cheerful. It was obvious that he was taking a new lease on life with Daphne out of the way. For a fleeting moment I wondered if he'd had anything to do with packing the kids off to ride herd on her. Then I saw his eyes slide uneasily toward Paula. No, if he'd had anything to do with it, he'd have got rid of Paula, too.

Paula looked as though she were going to say something to contest Hortense's claim for Horace's cleverness, but she seemed to change her mind. She just looked thoughtful.

They filed aboard the bus. I was almost the last aboard— and then I leaped the steps without even touching them as Jim smiled at me grimly.

She'd pinched me, too.

It was a peaceful ride back to London. The tourists were semicomatose from all that fresh air and their heavy tea. Without Daphne, there were no sudden stops or jerks.

Even I relaxed and stopped worrying about what Penny could have been hinting at so darkly. Obviously, she meant I was to phone her mother in case they met with an accident. But if Daphne wasn't driving, they were fairly safe. I didn't know how well Horace drove, but he couldn't have been worse than Daphne. If Daphne did regain the driving wheel, there were three of them to insist that she drive at a reasonable speed. There seemed to be nothing to worry over. Feeling almost like a tourist myself, I half-dozed on the way back to London.

•   •   •

Gerry was in the lobby when we entered the hotel. He looked at us all sharply, counting heads, but not finding the one he sought.

"Where's Daphne?" he demanded.

"On her way," I said.

"Why isn't she here yet?" The answer didn't satisfy him. "She should have been here ahead of you. She drives faster than that—even when she's being careful."

"I shouldn't be surprised"—Professor Tablor had come up behind us—"but what they've stopped off somewhere along the way." He chuckled indulgently. "That was probably the idea of the whole thing. It can't be much fun for the kids, stuck with a bunch of old codgers like us day in and day out. They've probably sneaked off to a discotheque for a couple of hours."

It was a reasonable theory, but I suddenly heard those bells crescendo again. It was too reasonable—Penny wouldn't have been so upset if that were all that was in the wind.

The party divided, some going upstairs to their rooms, some lingering hopefully near Gerry and me, as though we might suggest some fresh diversion for them. Fortunately, I knew that they were booked for Covent Garden that evening, so I didn't have too much of a conscience about ignoring them. Perhaps they'd take the hint and go away.

"She must be along soon." Gerry sat down firmly on the sofa. "She knows we have theatre tickets and it takes her a good hour to get ready. She'll be here any minute."

I sat down beside him, wondering why I didn't believe it. Perhaps because it was too pat. I found that I hadn't really believed that we were going to end this assignment so smoothly for some time now. But I could not say just when that nagging certainty of disaster had set in.

Through the plate-glass doors of the lobby, I could see Kate and Jim in conference on the pavement. Kate had the Covent Garden tickets, I knew, and Jim would drive them there and collect them after the performance. It was a 5:30 matinee and they'd have dinner afterward and be back at the hotel in time to pack for the morning departure. Although the plane officially left at 11:30, they had to check in at the airport an hour ahead of that, and if I knew Neil, he'd allow them plenty of time to get to the airport. At latest, they'd be leaving the hotel at 9:45.

Everything was under control, so why were my nerves strung up to screaming pitch?

Screaming. At first, I thought I'd cracked under the strain, then realised I could never hit a note that high. A series of short, sharp shrieks was coming from the direction of the descending lift, while a high banshee wailing was approaching via the staircase.

Hortense and Paula converged on the lobby at approximately the same moment and headed toward me.

"My baby!" Hortense shrieked. "My baby!"

"They've gone," Paula howled. "That dirty, rotten little Limey bitch is driving them to Gretna Green. They've eloped! You've got to *do* something!"

CHAPTER
THIRTEEN

PANDORA AWOKE, STARTLED AND MUTTERING CROSSLY, MOVED over to Gerry's shoulder, as though it might be more peaceful over there. Kate and Jim hurried into the lobby, their faces anxious. The other members of the tour began gathering around us.

"*Do* something," Hortense took up the cry. "That terrible creature has got her clutches on my baby."

"*My* baby," Paula countered sharply, "has been snatched away by that appalling lout. They'll be married if we don't hurry."

"Ladies, ladies," I said, "don't panic—" One of them hit me. It was too fast for me to be able to say which one, so I decided to rise above it.

"Nothing can happen that quickly," I said, shaking my head to clear it. "They changed that ruling years ago. It's just like the rest of Britain now. You have to establish residency for three weeks before you can get married in Gretna Green." (Trust Daphne, I thought grimly, not to know that. She'd been filling their heads with romantic notions that had no basis in reality.)

"What are they talking about?" Gerry appealed to me. He knew but didn't want to admit the knowledge to himself.

"Daphne"—I made him face it squarely—"is helping Donna and Horace to elope. She had no intention of coming back to London tonight—none of them did."

Suddenly, it was crystal clear. The way Daphne had made a deliberate nuisance, not to say menace, of herself on the roads. So that everyone would welcome the idea of the kids going off with her to try to keep her out of our way.

That—another light dawned—was what Penny had been trying to tell me.

"You mean"—Gerry's voice was hushed with the enormity of it all—"that Daphne has been interfering with our clients?"

"She's been just about as interfering as she can get," I assured him.

"Go after them," Paula shrieked. "We've got to catch them and stop them."

"Yes." For once, Hortense was in agreement with Paula. "We've got to stop them. Now!"

"Easy, girls, easy." Professor Tablor tried to intervene. "It isn't that bad, now. You heard what Douggie said. They can't get married there for three weeks."

"Yes," Hortense said darkly, "but what will they be *doing* during those three weeks?"

"That depends"—I tried for a note of cheerful sanity—"on the way you've brought them up, doesn't it?"

This time, they both hit me. It was nice, I supposed, that they agreed about something at last. If the worst happened, there'd be at least one meeting point at future family reunions. They could sit together and curse the son-of-a-bitch Limey who'd been partly responsible for it all.

With glazed detachment, I saw a chip of plaster from Paula's cast slide down my face and into my breast pocket. I was cad enough to hope that it had hurt her worse than it had hurt me, although that would have taken some doing. That cast was heavy—there was every chance I had a concussion. If she hadn't at least dislocated the broken arm trying to mend inside that cast, there was no justice.

Kate and Jim had closed with the situation now and were trying to sort it out. Hortense and Paula were still broadcasting on ultrahigh frequency. In a minute, we were going to be asked to leave the lobby, if not the hotel.

"We've got to find them. Stop them!" Paula was gesturing with that broken arm, the cast coming perilously close to clonking someone else. She didn't seem to be in any pain at all; there was obviously no justice.

On the other hand, I didn't seem to be concussed, after all. It was rather a pity. I could have used a good concussion and the honourable withdrawal to a darkened room and the peace and quiet it would have provided.

As it was, I'd just have to get up and struggle on.

"If we could catch up with them before they get to Gretna Green," Kate said thoughtfully, "that would be best. Once they cross that border, they've all of Scotland to disappear in."

It was basically correct, but not a thought I would have voiced aloud. Winnie and Billie Mae moved restively, as though reminded of another missing member of the tour.

"Come on," Paula said. "What are we waiting for? Let's get going!"

"Hurry!" Hortense urged. It was something else they were finally agreed upon.

"I don't know," Kate looked dubious. "I'll have to call Neil—"

"If you get him, let me know." I moved toward the sedan chair phone box with her. Jim came along, too.

"I don't know," he said. "I don't think I can stand it. The thought of getting rid of them for a few hours tonight was all that kept me going today."

"Think what will happen if they don't catch up with the kids," I said. "They'll cancel their return flight—Hortense and Paula will, at least. You'll have them around for days more, perhaps weeks."

"'Strewth!" He paled.

"And they'll expect Larkin's Luxury Tours to take care of them all the way." Ruthlessly I pressed home the advantage. "A private chauffeur, at least, to drive them around Scotland looking for the kids. They already know you—and you know how Americans love to stick with someone they know."

I wouldn't have thought it possible, but he went even paler. "We've got to do something." He caught up with the consensus in one giant stride. "We've got to catch those little bleeders before they get away."

Over his shoulder, I could see Kate dialing desperately once more. Wherever Neil was, we couldn't wait much longer to contact him. We were going to have to take this decision on our own.

It seemed to me that there was something I ought to do about telephoning, but my head had settled down to a deep, insistent throbbing, and it was more than I could face. How could I ring up Penny's mother and break it to her that her daughter had decamped with an eloping couple and might not surface again for three weeks? That's the sort of news mothers are notoriously unsympathetic about receiving. I couldn't face the questions—especially when I didn't have any explanations.

"I can't get him." Kate came out of the sedan chair with a harassed look. "The operator tried, too. There's no one there."

"And there are too many here," Jim muttered.

"We'll have to get started," I reminded them, "if we want to get out of London ahead of the rush-hour traffic. If we get caught in that, we'll be delayed for hours."

"I suppose," she agreed reluctantly, "there's really nothing else to do."

"Not unless Larkin's Luxury Tours wants a lawsuit for damages on its hands," I assured her. "Paula may not be able to collect, but it could cost everyone a lot in time and money while she tried."

We rejoined the ladies—and Paula and Hortense, too. The men were conferring with Gerry some distance away. They came back to the tour group when they saw us.

"Jim"—I clapped a firm hand on his shoulder, just in case he tried to bolt at the last minute—"has kindly volunteered to drive us to Gretna Green—on his own time— to see if we can't catch up with the kids along the way."

"That's lovely of you." There was a catch in Paula's voice, but there was usually a catch in anything to do with Paula. "Really lovely. I'll pay you back someway, I promise you."

Jim flinched and tried to back away, but I held him firm.

"I'm coming, too," Gerry said. "I have a few urgent matters to take up with Daphne." He hesitated. "I've a couple of theatre tickets I won't be needing. If any of you . . . ?" He offered them casually.

"And here"—Kate dug into her handbag—"are the Covent Garden tickets for tonight—" She broke off as she looked up and saw Professor Tablor shaking his head.

"No, thank you." As usual, he was spokesman for the group. "We've all come this far together, we'll stay together. We couldn't abandon our friends in their hour of need." Around him the others nodded agreement.

Translated, they still didn't trust one another out of each other's sight.

Gerry moved closer to me uneasily. "I've heard of American togetherness," he murmured, "but this is ridiculous."

He didn't know the half of it—and I wasn't going to tell him just yet. One accessory after the fact in Perkins & Tate (Public Relations) Ltd. was enough.

We broke free of London and hit the motorway just ahead of the flood tide of rush-hour traffic. Jim put his foot down to the floorboard, kept to the takeover lane, and we shot toward Scotland as though all the hounds of hell were yapping at our heels.

Even so, it wasn't fast enough for Hortense and Paula.

"Can't you get any more speed out of this thing?" Paula demanded. "They're hours ahead of us. We'll never catch them this way."

"We can't sprout wings," Jim muttered.

"What was that?" Ever alert for insubordination, Hortense whirled on him.

"I don't think you ought to distract the driver," I said hastily. "He's doing his best, and he needs to concentrate on the road."

Daggers drawn, Hortense and Paula glared at each other across the aisle, the picture of opposing in-laws at every wedding I had attended for the past ten years. Only the aisle was different; and of course, there was Jim officiating at the driving wheel. The bridal couple were missing, too, although we stood a good chance of catching up with them if we continued at this speed. All that was lacking were a couple of the misty relatives who always cried at weddings. Glancing in the rearview mirror, I saw that some of the tourists looked as though they might burst into tears at any moment, less from sentiment than from sheer terror at the way we were shooting past everything else on the motorway.

I turned around casually, to verify the fact that Professor Tablor seemed hale and hearty despite all the excitement. There never had been time to do any reading up on the care and feeding of diabetics, but he appeared to be holding up well. Of course, he'd had a good lunch and tea, and the tin of orange juice was still in my briefcase, in the event of an emergency. Just the same, it might be a good idea to make sure that we stopped for a snack somewhere along the way. Paula and Hortense might cavil at what they'd consider a waste of time, but it would pay off in goodwill all around. The others were missing Covent Garden, their last evening in London, and a chance for leisurely packing—there was no need for them to miss a meal, too. Daphne's lead was so great that half an hour or so wouldn't make that much difference. Besides, knowing how much of a start they'd gained on any possible pursuit, there was every good chance that the kids would take time to treat themselves to a good meal. In the sort of place Daphne would insist was fit to eat in, that could take two hours. There'd be no snatched motorway hamburgers for her.

The signs flashing past informed us that refreshment areas were two miles and twenty-seven miles ahead. Also telephones.

"Pull up at the next one, Jim," Kate directed. "I want to

try Neil again. He'll have to know where we're going and what's happening."

"We don't have time to stop," Paula snapped. "Keep going, Jim!"

That did it. Anxious though he was to be rid of her, Jim wasn't taking orders from her, even in so worthy a cause. He flicked on his directional signal and veered across the motorway into the turnoff lane.

"Don't you dare stop!" Paula snarled.

"Now, now," Tris Tablor tried to mediate, "we've been making very good time. I'm sure we can spare a few minutes for telephone calls and—"

"You mind your own business!" Paula whirled on him. "Nobody asked you to come along. You shoved yourself in on this—all of you—so if you don't like it, you can just lump it!"

"Personally," Hortense said coldly, "I welcome the presence of friends at a time like this. It's all in what you're accustomed to, of course. And I certainly don't begrudge them a few minutes to relax. I'm sure we'll all be the better for a cup of coffee—"

"You can talk—you've got nothing to lose!"

"My only son—" Hortense bridled.

"Your nasty little fortune hunter, who's taking advantage of an innocent young girl—"

"Your scheming little minx has deliberately ensnared my sweet, inexperienced boy—"

"Hah!" Paula said.

"What do you mean by that?"

"Hah! That's all—just hah!"

Jim pulled into the parking lot behind the restaurant and slammed on the brakes with finality. We all lurched forward and rocked back again. Paula struck her cast on the back of my seat but was so anaesthetised by fury that she didn't seem to notice it.

"You can't stop," she screamed. "You can't! They're getting farther away all the time."

"*I* don't mind if we stop," Hortense said coldly, "and I'm quite as anxious to catch up with them as you are."

"I'll bet," Paula snarled. "I'll just bet!"

"Yes, you can bet on it," Hortense said. "I've other plans for my son. I want him to marry a lady. A refined girl, with good breeding—"

"Don't hand me that," Paula said. "You've probably been egging him on all the while. I've heard those kids talking together, and I know my Donna—she never could keep anything to herself."

Hortense paled. I couldn't tell whether it was with outrage or guilt. But guilt was a word I didn't want to think about. It could explain a lot about this latest episode. A wife can't be forced to testify against her husband—and vice versa. Did the same hold true for mothers and mothers-in-law? Were the kids trying to protect each other? Or one of their mothers?

I turned around, hoping I was raking them with a casual glance. Hortense and Horace came from the same town as Carrie—who knew what animosities were concealed beneath Hortense's cool exterior? She was a lady who clung to her dignity, perhaps at any price. Horace was at the age when he might be experimenting with drugs—and he might have got involved with Carrie's protégé that way. Perhaps they shared the same pusher. And Carrie was a harsh and unforgiving woman, with a blind spot only for the weaknesses of her protégé—and the fury of a lioness protecting her cub, which she turned against anyone who seemed to threaten him in any way. It was easy to imagine her and Hortense clashing head-on over their respective young. And knowing Hortense, it was easy to imagine her winning. Of course, I'd never seen Carrie, but if she had been more formidable than Hortense, I was just as glad I hadn't.

On the other hand, Paula could easily be a murderer. For the simple reason that she was so obnoxious that, if anyone was to be murdered in Tour 79, she should have been first choice for victim. Since she wasn't, it was easier to imagine her as the murderer, instead. There wasn't the long background of living in the same town as the victim, but given the sort of women they both were, need there have been? Mutual hate, from the first moment of introduction, could have sprung up between them, intensifying across Europe until it erupted in murder.

There was just one little thing wrong with that idea. I rubbed my still-aching head ruefully. Paula favoured direct action and would have been more likely to have a go at Carrie with a steak knife than to bide her time, hold her tongue, and play games with pills.

". . . all about it," Paula was saying as I forced my concentration back to the moment. "Sooner or later, she tells everyone. It's been preying on her mind ever since she learned the terms of the settlement. That's why I have to watch her so carefully. To keep her from pulling just this damned foolish stunt she's trying to pull now. To keep her from making the same mistake I did—getting married too young."

"I agree"—Hortense was tight-lipped—"that it would be a most serious mistake. I'm not anxious for Horace to make it, either."

"The hell you're not!" Paula snarled. "You and your precious son have your eyes on that half a million dollars—

just like everybody else my poor, stupid baby shoots her mouth off to."

"Half a million dollars?" Hortense said faintly.

"Don't try to pretend you didn't know. That louse—my first husband, Donna's father—settled half a million dollars in a trust for her, separate from the settlement he made on me. She gets it when she's twenty-five, or when she marries—whichever comes first.

"So, you see"—Paula turned desperately to Jim, who had switched off the ignition, removed the keys, and put them in his pocket—"we've got to go on. If she gets married, I'll never see it—her—again."

"Sorry." Jim pushed the lever opening the door. "We'll take twenty minutes 'ere. The place is licensed. 'Ave a drink."

He was the first one out of the bus. Unhesitatingly he marched through the door labeled "Gentlemen." There was no arguing with that one.

As the rest of us filed thankfully off the bus, Paula sat back in her seat. She tried to fold her arms and seemed rather surprised by the cast, which got in her way.

CHAPTER

FOURTEEN

"MR. PERKINS"—THE VOICE OF PENNY'S MOTHER WAS FAINT, but determined—"are you certain my daughter is perfectly safe?"

I began to wish that I hadn't made that telephone call, after all. But it was growing late, and I thought I'd better ring and say that Penny was working late. If her mother had gotten worried and tried to call our office, she'd have worried even more at getting no answer.

"Penny called me at four from Dunstable and said to tell you they were heading north. She called again at five-thirty" —there was a rustling of papers—"to say they were at Tamworth and turning onto the M-six. Then"—there was more rustling—"she rang—she seemed most upset that you hadn't contacted me yet—to say they were stopping for dinner in Preston. That was about an hour ago. She expected to be there about an hour and a half, and then they planned to rejoin the M-six and keep heading north. Mr. Perkins"—her voice sharpened—"they seemed to be making exceptionally fast time between those points. Are you certain Penny is perfectly safe?"

How I'd love to know the answer to that one myself. But Penny's mother didn't want the truth, she wanted reassurance.

"I promise you," I said, crossing my fingers, "Penny is in no danger." I hoped I was right.

"Mr. Perkins"—she was still dubious—"you haven't taken on a racing driver as a client, have you?"

"No, we haven't." That, at least, I could answer with complete honesty. Daphne might drive as though every road were the Indianapolis Speedway, but she wasn't technically a racing driver—and she certainly wasn't a client.

"What *is* happening?" The voice grew plaintive. "Penny won't tell me. She just says she hasn't time to answer questions. *What* are you *doing?* Where are you *going?*"

Outside, I could see Tour 79 boarding the bus again. It was unfortunate for Penny's mother, but I didn't have time to answer questions, either.

"Sorry," I said, "I must go now. If Penny rings again, tell her she's doing a great job. Tell her to stall them all she can, and to keep her chin up. We'll try to head them off at the pass."

"What pass? What are you talking—?"

"Sorry, good-bye," I said, and rang off.

Paula was in a definite snit as we reentered the bus. The others were looking infinitesimally more relaxed (thank heavens the place was licensed), although still not completely happy. I began to suspect that some of them might even have preferred Covent Garden. At least, they'd still have been in the centre of London and not speeding through the growing dusk with no clear idea of when they'd see their beds again.

Jim lurked outside until the very last minute, then leaped aboard and started the engine with an expression so forbidding that even Paula hesitated to say anything to him.

I'd bagged the seat immediately behind him and gave him the information I'd received from Penny's mother. He nodded grimly, assimilating it and calculating our chances of catching up with them, then gave his verdict.

"If we can keep moving, and they slow down a bit, maybe a couple of hours. If we don't get delayed. If they don't decide to change course. If—"

"Just do your best," I said. "Remember the alternative." The alternative was having Paula and the rest of Tour 79 hung around our necks like albatrosses for an indefinite period.

"Right!" He pushed the accelerator down against the floorboard again, and we took off like a souped-up rocket.

Motorways are alike everywhere; only the notice boards vary to give you a clue which country you're in. Tour 79 had settled down to their usual silent withdrawal from the situation—any situation—they found themselves in. Or perhaps—I tried to be kind—highway hypnosis had set in. The silence was oppressive; only the throb of the motor provided a background noise as we moved inexorably forward into the gathering night.

We were making good time. I looked at the speedometer once and avoided it thereafter. I'd rather not know. As the American cop said, giving out a ticket, "You weren't driving too fast, you were flying too low."

But Jim knew what he was doing, and the bus was in

control—so long as no one distracted him and the road remained clear and free of obstructions.

Penny would do all she could, too. I knew that. I should have listened to her, but I'd thought she wanted to tell me more about the death of Carrie in Zurich, and I'd heard enough about that. Penny was not only bright, she had a good sense of responsibility as well. Look at the way she had handed Pandora back to me, unwilling to trust her to Daphne's driving.

Pandora was lying on Gerry's chest now as he half-reclined against the seat, brooding. They were nose-to-nose in silent communion. Pandora was purring. Gerry, I was willing to bet, was mentally rehearsing what he was going to say to Daphne when we caught up with her. If we caught up with her.

Meanwhile, the natives were growing restless. I heard Paula stir behind us and the thump of her cast against the window, as though she was trying to settle into a more comfortable position. She ought to be glad that the weather was so cool; that cast would have been more uncomfortable in a heat wave. I wondered again who could have pushed her—remembering that she had been strangely silent after the first accusation, and that Donna had been closest to her when she fell. Had Donna hoped for a broken leg to immobilize her mother while she eloped? Or had she hoped for a more serious injury? Paula was controlling the income from the trust fund—if anything happened to her, perhaps Donna wouldn't have to marry to get control of her own money.

Yet Donna hadn't seemed positive enough to be so calculating. She seemed more the victim type. Whereas Paula was a definite predator.

Outside, the signposts flashed past. Driving lights were

being switched on now and cat's eyes glowed, marking the borders of the road. We were gaining on the others—provided that they weren't going as fast as we were. Even for Daphne, that seemed unlikely.

I wondered if Penny had managed to engineer another stop yet, to report progress to her mother. If so, she'd know that we were on the way. It was time Perkins & Tate gave her a bonus—driving with Daphne called for danger money, even when she wasn't racing to get across borders—and Neil Larkin could damn well foot the bill for it. These were his chestnuts we were pulling out of the fire, after all.

There was a faint murmur from somewhere behind me. I couldn't distinguish the whisperer, but I heard the wistful word "home." It would be what they were all wondering. Whether or not they were going to get back to London in time to pack and catch their plane tomorrow. The way they must be feeling at this moment, it would be the only luxury Larkin's Luxury Tours could provide for them that they cared about. When they did reach their distant homes, and friends dropped round to hear all about their trip, what would they tell them? Would time soften their memories, as Neil had hoped, so that they would look at the photographs in the local rag, read the enthusiastic write-up, and actually believe they'd had such a good time?

On the other hand, they'd have to carry out the charade to some extent. They couldn't break down and admit, "Well, it was a pretty good tour, barring a spot of murder in Switzerland. Of course, we all clammed up about that and the cops never found out." No, there were still laws about murder and conspiracy. There were extradition treaties, too. They couldn't afford themselves the luxury of admit-

ting how unluxurious their tour had really been. Neil
might just be lucky there.

We had the motorway nearly to ourselves now. The last
turnoff had funneled off the stream of late home-goers
behind us. Coming toward us, a lien of cars veered sharply
into their turnoff. The night suddenly seemed darker than
before. With our increasing isolation on the road, restiveness
became more apparent among the members of Tour 79.

The sight of so many people headed for the privacy and
comfort of their homes obviously reminded them of their own
positions. They must feel like Flying Dutchmen, at this
point, condemned to wander the world unceasingly for their
sins. When would they see their own homeland and homes
again? If we didn't catch up with the kids before they went
to ground in some tiny lodging house, who knew?

From across the aisle came a not-very-strangled sob. I
tried to ignore it. Maternal hysterics were all we needed just
now. I preferred Paula's belligerency. At least it could be
more easily dealt with.

Perhaps, I cheered up slightly, their moods would cancel
each other out. The best cure for hysterics was a good slap
in the face—and my money was on Paula to administer it. It
would come better from her than from any of us; furthermore, she'd enjoy doing it.

The worst of hysteria is that it can be contagious. From
somewhere behind us came the sound of a long, quavering
breath. Nerves that had had too much to cope with over the
past few weeks were nearing a breaking point. Tension
swirled through the bus like a tangible force—nerves could
not be allowed to break. That way lay confession—and the
confession of one person could trap them all.

But Hortense was not going to be upstaged by anyone
else. She obviously felt, with some justification, that she

had a better right to hysterics than someone with nothing so personal at stake. She drew a quavering breath of her own and launched out on a keening tirade.

"I brought my son up to be a gentleman. He was the best student in his class, he was going to college next year. I never thought he'd throw himself away on a little—"

"You can't complain," Paula cut in. "He's latched on to a good thing. My poor little Donna is making just the mistake I made when I was her age."

They might at least count their blessings. I wouldn't say they weren't losing a child because, if those kids had half the sense I gave them credit for, they'd keep well away from their doting parents. But the mothers had each gained a sparring partner.

"Ladies, ladies." Only Professor Tablor, determined to be peacemaker, would rush in where the rest of us had no intention of treading. "Why don't you try to understand each other's point of view? After all, you have a lot in common, both being widow ladies, of a sort—"

"Don't you put me in the same class with her!" Hortense whirled on him. "She's nothing but a grass widow; whereas, I"—she drew herself up proudly—"am a *sod* widow!"

The bus lurched sharply. "It's all right," I said to Jim. I'd heard the expression before in the States. "She just means she buried her husband, and Paula divorced hers."

"Gawdstrewth," Jim moaned softly, "you never can tell with these bleedin' Yanks!"

"Listen, I'll have you know. . ." Paula began.

Ahead of us, beyond a bend in the road, we could see flashing blue lights. They conveyed nothing to the tourists, but Gerry and I exchanged glances. Jim slowed down.

The others suddenly grew quiet, as though sensing more trouble impending. The unerring magnet of disaster drew their eyes to the windows. We bore down on the scene in silence.

A policeman with a torch was waving traffic past. He signaled furiously at us, but we had recognised the white wreckage. Jim pulled the bus to a stop behind the ambulance.

Faced with a genuine disaster, the women were quiet. It must have been like this, that night in Switzerland. Eyes met eyes in the silent bus, sporadically illuminated by the flashing blue lights outside, and the tacit message sounded through the bus as clearly as though it had been spoken: *Battle stations.*

Tristan Tablor moved up to the front of the bus to stand behind Hortense and Paula, who were waiting on the steps for Jim to pull the release lever and open the door.

The others stood and moved out into the aisle, closing ranks, allied again in the face of an emergency. The shuttered faces, the relentlessness of their forward surge, made them seem suddenly formidable.

It was easy to see how they had defied and defeated any police investigation in Switzerland.

With a hiss of compressed air, the door opened and Hortense, Paula, and Tristan leaped to the ground. Gerry and I weren't far behind them—Penny had been in that car, too.

It hadn't caught on fire—at least there was that. The wreckage was a Chinese puzzle of twisted metal, another car inextricably entwined with the Lancia. In the flashing blue lights, white paint glimmered faintly on no-longer-recognisable components. I had no consciousness of breathing at all as we covered the last few yards, ignoring the people who tried to stop us. It took a moment to pull my eyes away from the wreckage and scan the surrounding scene. That was when I noticed my breathing, because I resumed it just then.

It's amazing what people can walk away from. The kids were huddled together on the grass verge, romance nowhere in their thoughts now. (If it had ever been. There was every good chance that the escapade had been planned as much to spite their mothers as to consummate any great love. With the added advantage to Donna of gaining control of her own money.)

Penny was sitting down at their feet. She looked groggy. I covered the remaining distance with a standing broad jump. "Are you all right?"

She considered this question with the seriousness it deserved. "I think so. Shaken. But we all had our seat belts fastened. And it wasn't," she added wonderingly, "even Daphne's fault."

I didn't believe that, but I let it go and looked round for a doctor. They might think they were all right, but I'd rather have a professional opinion on the subject. Just to be sure.

I wasn't the only one. While the mothers were reclaiming their darlings, Tris Tablor had found the doctor.

"They *are* all right?" he was insisting. "They are *perfectly* all right? They weren't unconscious, or irrational from shock or anything?"

The others clustered eagerly behind him, listening for the reassuring answers. The doctor must have considered them very thoughtful, sympathetic people, touchingly anxious about the younger members of their tour. He couldn't know that the catch in the questioning was that bit about being irrational. They wanted to be sure that the kids hadn't talked. Hadn't said anything, under the influence of shock, or any drugs that might have been administered, to give the game away.

"And it will be all right for them to travel?" Still grimly earnest, Tablor persisted. "We're flying home tomorrow.

They can come with us? It won't be dangerous for them to
fly? It won't hurt them in any way?"

Again, the answers were reassuring. The kids were shak-
en, bruised, they'd be feeling sore and aching for a few
days, perhaps longer, but there was nothing to stop them
from boarding an airliner, settling back in those reclining
seats, and resting all the way home. Although, it would be
safest if they had their own doctors examine them later—a
couple of ribs might be cracked, rather than merely bruised.
But basically, they were the luckiest young people alive—to
have come through that crash in no worse condition.

There was a mass exhalation of relief. What nice people
the doctor must have thought them, so concerned about their
young friends. So pleased not to be losing them as traveling
companions.

So relieved not to have to leave anyone behind who might
blurt out the truth about Tour 79 in an incautious moment.

I turned away abruptly. Gerry had found Daphne. She
was still exchanging particulars and recriminations with the
driver of the other car, a policeman acting as referee. Both
cars were a complete write-off. It was going to be an
interesting case for their respective insurance companies.

Pandora twisted unhappily in Gerry's arms; he was keeping too tight a grip on her, perhaps for fear of her running
away in the midst of all the excitement. Or perhaps, in his
annoyance at Daphne, he was unaware of squeezing poor
Pandora.

Out of the corner of my eye, I saw Kate Lamb trying to
herd the tourists back into the bus. Hortense and Paula,
having pulled their dazed and unresisting progeny well
apart, were already urging them toward the bus, more
anxious than anyone to make that morning flight to home
and safety.

"And where *were* you?" Daphne whirled suddenly on Gerry. "If you were going to come chasing after us, why couldn't you have got here sooner? This is all," she wound up, in a triumph of female logic, "*your* fault!"

Pandora yowled, and I stepped forward and pried her out of Gerry's grasp. As he took a deep breath for rebuttal, I walked away and left them to it. Gerry could handle this by himself. I had my own problems to see to.

Pandora muttered complaints as I tried to soothe her, walking swiftly back to Penny, who was still sitting on the grass verge.

"Here." I dumped Pandora into her arms, then scooped her up and made for the bus. "Excuse me." I shouldered my way between Hortense and Paula and their offspring, reaching the bus half a length ahead of them. The door was open; I boarded and marched straight down the aisle, bagging the full-length back seat and stretching Penny out on it.

When I turned around, both Hortense and Paula were glaring at me. Each of them had had that seat in mind for the comfort of her child. The hell with them—it was their fault that Penny had been injured. I glared back, and after a moment, they turned away to settle Donna and Horace into side seats.

Some of the others began to straggle aboard. "It shouldn't be too long before we get moving," I told Penny. "Anything you want?"

Meanwhile, Pandora had made her own diagnosis and decided on treatment. She began to wash Penny's chin.

Penny giggled faintly and shook her head. "It tickles," she said, closing her eyes. She fell asleep then, or passed out. But she seemed basically all right, and she needed some rest.

I took the aisle seat immediately in front of her and

settled down. Probably I should have been out there helping Kate Lamb, but Jim was with her. Gerry was giving every indication of leaving Daphne and doing something useful, as well.

I stayed where I was, telling myself that Penny might awaken and want something. Not even to myself was I willing to admit that I was really guarding her.

CHAPTER
FIFTEEN

IN THE DARKENED BUS, WE SPED QUIETLY BACK TO LONDON. NO one felt like talking. Hortense and Paula—the ones with the most to be said about this episode—had to wait until their proper audience was conscious and stronger. They brooded out of their respective windows, Paula chain-smoking, both of them turning occasionally to check on their chicks.

The rest of Tour 79 tried to doze. They'd better. They'd have precious few hours of the luxury of a hotel bed tonight—and there was still all their packing to be done. By now, there was one prevailing mood, one overriding ambition shared by everyone in the bus: Tour 79 was going to be on that plane in the morning. Or rather, later this morning. . . .

The night porter at the hotel opened the door to us, after allowing a decent interval for us to change our minds and go away. When we unsportingly kept ringing the bell, he let us in.

Neil was waiting in the lobby, looking worse than any of us—and that was saying quite a lot. He struggled forward, out of the armchair he had been occupying, and was nearly knocked back into it as Kate flew into his arms. He patted her on the shoulder, slipped aside, and lowered her into the armchair, with a dexterity Gerry might have envied, then came to meet the rest of us. I didn't like his expression.

He didn't look as though he liked our expressions, or us at all, either. We were tired, travel-stained, nerve-frayed, and longing for sleep. So was he. He looked us over and gave it to us straight, not bothering to try to soften the blow.

"The police think they've found our missing tourist," he said. "They pulled her out of the Thames yesterday. They want someone who knew her to come and identify the body."

Tour 79 drew together into a tight defensive unit. It was only apparent when you looked closely that none of them were actually touching one another. They were united, yet withdrawn; dependent on each other, but mistrustful. Gradually, heads turned until one person was the focus of attention.

"Yes." With a deep sigh, Tristan Tablor accepted the responsibilities of command. He had been morale officer, cheerleader, fun-and-games director; now it was time to shoulder the graver duties one's subordinates expected of an officer and a gentleman. "Yes, I guess I knew her as well as anybody here. I guess it's up to me to see to this."

Neil nodded, looking beyond him, to Jim. "We'll never find a taxi at this hour—can you drive us?"

"'Strewth, and I complained about the hours in London Transport!" But he was already turning toward the door. Looking slightly dazed, Tris Tablor followed him.

"I'd suggest the rest of you try to get some sleep," Neil said, dismissing the others, who were still standing together indecisively. Glazed with fatigue, some of them began straggling toward the lifts.

"The police will want to talk to everyone first thing in the morning." Neil walked back to Kate and bent over her. Gerry and I had gone with him, foolishly hoping we might get a bit more information that he felt the tourists were entitled to. Penny trailed behind us, half-asleep, still clutching Pandora as, a couple of years ago, she might have clutched her favourite teddy bear.

"It will be simplest if you stay the rest of the night here." Neil swung to face us. "I've taken a suite. You can share it with Kate."

It seemed like the most reasonable solution. We'd have trouble getting transport at this hour, too. Then there was Penny. I didn't want to be the one to deliver her to her anxious mother at this time of the morning. It would be much easier to remain here and let Penny telephone that she was safe and well and would return home later in the day.

I wasn't the only one worrying about Penny. Paula had come up behind us and tapped Penny on the shoulder.

"I was just thinking," she said, in improbably honeyed tones, "I suppose I ought to thank you. If you hadn't kept in contact and left messages, we'd never have known where to find them. They might have got away."

"Oh, that's all right." Penny smiled sweetly. "We have to look after the interests of our clients, you know. It's all part of the job."

"I suppose that's true," Paula said slowly. "Just the same, it was awfully nice of you." Donna was waiting for her over by the lift, she'd said her thank-you, and still she lingered. She put out her hand and stroked Pandora thoughtfully. Pandora laid her ears back and watched her warily through narrowed eyes. That was rather the way I felt. I edged nearer.

"I suppose," Paula continued, a trifle too casually, "you kids did a lot of laughing and talking together. I mean, you were together for hours. I suppose you talked about all kinds of things—"

That was enough. I bore down on them, sweeping Penny away. "Time to get some rest. There's a busy day ahead of us, once the sun comes up. You girls can gossip later."

Gerry had caught part of what was happening, although he had been listening to Kate and Neil until Neil left. He gave me a questioning look as he walked to the lift with us, escorting Kate tenderly. (I was glad that she was safely spoken for.) I ignored it, as I tried to ignore the knowledge of Paula's eyes boring balefully into my receding back.

The suite was something to see—Neil had done us proud. If I'd been able to identify period antiques, I'm sure I'd have been impressed. Gerry whistled softly, but I concentrated on the essentials. There were two bedrooms, both with twin beds, with excellent innerspring mattresses—no nonsense about keeping in period here. The bathroom contained toothbrushes and an electric shaver, I was glad to see. There wasn't much point in going to bed now, but a shower and a shave would help a bit.

Kate and Penny took over one of the bedrooms, and Penny rang her mother before falling asleep again. Very thoughtfully, she rang from the bedroom and shut the door. My nerves weren't up to hearing any part of that conversation, especially not Penny's one-sided defense of her situation. Her mother was either an extremely long-suffering person, or Penny had an iron determination beneath that fluffy exterior—otherwise, we'd have been looking for a new secretary long since.

Pandora had slept well in the bus and was wide-awake now—the only one of us who was. She prowled around the sitting room with interest, sniffing into the corners and checking the windowsills, always glancing back at us to make sure that we were still there. She needn't have worried; we were too exhausted to go anywhere else.

She was a game little cat, though. Always happy exploring new places—and no nonsense about butter on her paws to settle her down. Or perhaps it was just that we were all there with her. Me, Gerry, and Penny. So long as she was with her people, she was content.

"Prrah!" She jumped up on the sofa between us, bright-eyed, and looked expectantly from one to the other. She was ready for something to happen. Food, games, petting, it didn't matter which.

We were disappointing company. We sprawled there, in the last stages of exhaustion, not even enough strength to lift a hand and stroke her. She began to upbraid us.

"It's indecent," Gerry said. "No creature should have that much energy at this hour of the morning."

"She can't help it," I said. "She's a lot smaller than we are. It doesn't take so long for her to restore her strength."

"It will take me," he said firmly, "at least twenty-four hours." He paused and considered. "Perhaps thirty-six."

"Which, unfortunately, we are unlikely to have clear for some time yet." I pulled my handkerchief out of my pocket. The chip from Paula's cast came with it and bounced to the floor.

With a pleased cry, Pandora bounded after it. This was more like it—something to play with. We hadn't failed her, after all.

She batted the chunk of plaster with one paw, sending it skittering across the carpet, and leaped to head it off before it landed in the corner. She whirled about and hit it again, knocking it back in our direction.

Gerry obligingly put out his foot and kicked it back to her. He was right—she was too energetic. It was a pity that some of that enthusiasm couldn't be harnessed and transferred to us. We could use it right now. Although Gerry seemed to have a bit more than me. Of course, he hadn't been on duty with Tour 79 as long as I had.

I watched them idly as they kicked the small, glittering object back and forth between them. Then my brain abruptly meshed into gear again.

Glittering?

I dived for the chunk of plaster. Pandora gave a welcoming yowl as I joined the game, then a snarl of protest as I settled back on the sofa clutching her new toy. I was being a miserable spoilsport again.

"What's the matter?" Gerry asked, puzzled, but alerted by my sudden interest.

I was chipping with my thumbnail at the plaster surrounding the glittering dot. Bright, multicoloured sparks shot from the depths of the plaster in the lamplight. Gerry whistled softly and moved closer, pulling out a penknife.

"Here"—he took the chunk of plaster away from me—"we can use this. Don't worry," he added as I winced, "you can't hurt *that* baby with a bit of steel."

He whittled away at the plaster with more enthusiasm than skill. Gradually, the shining stone emerged, slightly dulled by the bits of plaster still clinging to it, but identifiable.

"Well, well!" Gerry held the gem, point still embedded in the chunk of plaster, out at arm's length, admiring it. "They *are* using expensive materials in the National Health Service these days. No wonder rates keep going up."

"Oh, God," I groaned, "an uncut diamond. It needed only this."

"Tut, tut," Gerry clucked, "not uncut. Unset. It's very

nicely cut, indeed. Baguette cut, about half a carat, blue-white, and I'd say"——he twirled the plaster, watching the flashing sparks of light—"quite probably perfect."

"You're the expert." I accepted his correction. Gerry has been trailed past so many jewelry shop windows by hinting birds that he must know as much about it as anyone this side of Hatton Garden. As he has himself remarked, had he been born a century earlier, he could have worked up a nice sideline with Asprey's by hiring out as an extra hitching post, he'd been immobilized outside their windows by twittering birds so often and for such long periods.

"Hardly expert," he demurred modestly, "but it stands to reason, doesn't it? No use buying unset stones for invest-ment unless they *are* perfect. I assume they *are* for investment?"

"A nest egg," I agreed, "against the days when alimony isn't so easily come by, and the little bird in the nest grows old enough to fly away and manage her own money."

"And the bird is on the wing," Gerry said cheerfully. "Ah, yes, diamonds are a girl's best friend."

"I thought that cast looked awfully lumpy," I brooded. "No wonder she kept so quiet about her injury after the accident."

"That alone should have made us suspicious," Gerry said. "Not the stoic type, our Paula. We should have known better. But they're all a bit odd and unnatural—for tourists. Makes you wonder what some of the rest of them are hiding, doesn't it?"

I didn't say a word; I carefully kept my expression blank, but we'd known each other for too many years.

"Or does it?" He looked at me thoughtfully. "Doug, old boy, is there anything you ought to tell me?"

"You don't want to know," I said. "It would make you an

accessory after the fact. This way, just one of us could go to jail."

"Don't be too sure," he said. "Remember that great old legal maxim, 'In the eyes of the law, ignorance is no excuse.' They've got you coming and going. Besides, we might as well be cellmates, we're used to each other, and you wouldn't like some of the rough types they might toss you in with. You've lived too sheltered a life."

"I did until I went into PR." But Gerry was right, as usual. I spent the next half hour catching him up with the situation. At the end, he was looking considerably shaken.

"My, my"—he shook his head—"and they used to call them 'innocents abroad.' How times have changed."

Dawn was streaking the horizon outside the hotel window. I'm as fond of dawn as the next man—providing the next man is Gerry—but I felt I'd sat up and watched too many of them in the wrong company since Perkins & Tate (Public Relations) Ltd. had first set up in business. I thought wearily of the dreams we'd had when we started out—they included a staff to deal with the rough stuff, such as sitting up all night with clients, and an estate in the country, where the only time we'd greet the dawn would be with a champagne breakfast after a Hunt Club ball. In our youth and innocence, we reckoned we ought to reach those modest goals within a couple of years.

"We just have to hold out a few hours longer." I tried to cheer myself on, as much as Gerry. "They aren't going to crack now—too much is at stake. They ought to skim through the police questioning like a hot knife through butter—they've had plenty of practise in Switzerland. All they have to do is get on that plane and they're in the clear. Their only problem then is trying to live with their consciences. We can live with ours."

"You may be right," Gerry said. "You probably are. But"—he tossed the diamond-studded chunk of plaster into the air and caught it deftly—"what price noninvolvement if they're caught by Customs and Excise when they land on home territory? One question leads to another, you know. What would you consider a sporting wager on the probability of Paula's keeping a stiff upper lip if she thought she could lighten her sentence by shopping her associates?"

"I wouldn't give that chunk of plaster *without* the diamond."

"Right," Gerry said. He stood up and pocketed it. "In that case, it's back to the jolly old drawing board, isn't it? Shall we cut along and explain a few facts about International Commercial Courtesy to a certain lady?"

Paula answered the door. Like us, she hadn't bothered to try to sleep. I didn't for a moment think it was because her conscience was bothering her. Her nerves might be going a bit wonky as the moment of facing U.S. Customs grew nearer, but her conscience was ironclad in the certainty that she was in the right. It's the only way a smuggler can get away with it. Usually.

"Come in." She wasn't overjoyed to see us, but she had no reason to suspect anything, either. "Sit down." She swept an arm toward the two chairs. Unfortunately, it was the wrong arm. She realised this and shrugged.

"I'm trying to exercise it a little. So's it doesn't get too stiff." She had changed into a traveling suit, and a matching scarf was knotted into a sling around her neck in readiness. She slipped the cast into it. "I suppose I shouldn't overdo."

Donna was lying in one of the twin beds. She wasn't asleep, but she was pretending to be. If the alternative was a long conversation with Paula, I'd have done the same.

"You might do better if you went without it entirely," Gerry said. "The cast, I mean. In fact, I'd strongly recommend it."

"What do you mean?" She flared instantly. "Listen, you're lucky I don't sue. It was that lousy, unsafe, rickety-stepped joint your partner took us to that—"

Gerry tossed the chunk of plaster to her. She stopped in midsentence, catching it automatically. The diamond gleamed wickedly under the overhead light.

"So, okay." She glared at us defiantly. "So, what are you going to do about it?"

Donna sat up in bed, aware that something had happened and no longer able to continue the pretense of sleep. Paula didn't notice her.

"Nothing," Gerry answered for us both. "Because you aren't going to be so silly. You're going to take that cast off, chip the diamonds out of it, and declare them at Customs like a good little girl."

"And suppose I don't?"

"Then you'll be liable for a heavy fine, the diamonds and any other little baubles you've tucked away will be confiscated, and you might even face a jail sentence—depending, of course, on your general attitude during the proceedings."

Donna was smiling broadly. It was the first time I had seen her look even remotely happy during her entire sojourn in this country. Fortunately, her mother didn't turn around.

"You said you weren't going to do anything." Paula was as white as her homemade plaster cast.

"We don't need to." Gerry sighed deeply. "It was all done before you left the country of purchase, probably before you even left the shop."

"It was a diamond factory," she said. "Near Amsterdam."

"There's no difference, they're all in the agreement."

"What agreement?" She didn't want to believe, but Gerry's attitude was forcing her to, however reluctantly.

"Gentlemen's, perhaps," Gerry said. "All I know is that Continental jewelry shops automatically report all purchases over a certain modest amount to the Customs and Excise Department of the home country of any foreign purchaser. Then, if the purchaser doesn't declare the goods—"

"They wouldn't do that!" But she was no longer so sure of her ground as she had been.

"If they don't," Gerry said, "then one of the sales staff does. It makes a nice little supplementary income—I understand some of them are putting their children through very expensive schools on the bounty money."

"You mean our United States Customs Department listens to sneaks like that?"

"I believe they actually encourage them," Gerry said. "They give a reward of twenty-five percent of the value of the goods, up to a maximum of twenty thousand pounds. And of course, once the goods have been confiscated, you never get them back—not even after paying your fine. They're kept and sold at auction at some later date."

"Why the dirty, rotten, lousy sons-of-bitches!"

"Amen, amen," Gerry said sadly. "You can't trust anyone these days."

I dodged quickly as she made a sudden movement, but she had only hurled the chunk of plaster back at us. Gerry caught it deftly.

"Temper, temper," he said. "Don't forget there's a nice little diamond in that." He tried to hand it back to her.

"Keep it," she said. "It will be one less I have to pay duty on."

"No, no, I couldn't." He tossed it to her with instinctive revulsion. "I'm superstitious. Diamonds are bad luck."

"You're telling me," she said bitterly. She tried to throw it back, but he moved away. I stepped in and caught it. We'd saved her a lot of money in fines, not to mention the attendant unpleasantness. We could call it *our* reward for information.

"We'd better be getting along now," Gerry said. "You have quite a busy time ahead of you—chipping all your baubles out of their impromptu setting."

"Yeah." Paula sent him a look of pure hatred. Gerry flinched. He isn't used to getting those kind of looks from women. Oh, well, you can't win 'em all.

Donna lay back and pulled the covers over her head. I could see the bedclothes shaking uncontrollably. It was nice that someone was amused.

"Wait a minute," Paula said to me as we reached the door. She crossed to the suitcase open on her bed and pulled out a slightly wilted notebook.

"Here, give this back to the professor, would you?" She met my eyes and looked away. "I wasn't going to keep it, anyway," she said. "I'd have mailed it back to him later. But he had all that stuff in it about me spending so long shopping, and in the diamond factory and everything. If anyone had looked at it, going through customs, I thought—"

I took it. "I'll see that he gets it."

"And listen, you don't have to tell him where you got it, do you? I mean, you can just say you found it, or something."

She probably didn't deserve it, but I nodded. "Don't worry, I'll explain it someway."

We were nearly out the door when she said, "Hey, listen."

I turned around.

"Thanks" she said awkwardly.

CHAPTER SIXTEEN

GERRY APPLIED A BIT OF DISCREET BRIBERY IN THE RIGHT QUAR-
ters, and we got a pot of coffee and some sandwiches to
take back to our suite. Penny was up and playing with
Pandora when we got there.

Pandora sprang forward to twine around my ankles,
telling me how much she had missed me, and mentioning
only in passing that she'd been growing decidedly peckish.
Penny's face brightened at the sight of sustenance, too.

I took half a sandwich apart and started to put the side
with the clinging salmon mayonnaise down for Pandora. The
thick pile of the carpet gave me a sudden pang of conscience. Although Pandora was usually a very tidy eater,
this could be the one time she wasn't. There was nothing
else around, so I put the exercise book down and set the
open sandwich on top. Purring with satisfaction, Pandora
crouched over it eagerly. If she slopped a bit, the professor

would forgive her. What are a few grease spots between friends?

Gerry was pouring coffee while I settled Pandora. The sofa would be overcrowded with three, so I stayed on the floor beside Pandora and helped myself to the other half of her sandwich. Gerry passed down a cup of coffee to me.

There was a short silence while we all concentrated on food. Pandora finished first and prowled over to thrust her muzzle into my second sandwich, nearly abstracting the slice of ham. I took the hint and found another salmon sandwich for her.

We were finishing the last of the coffee when I pulled the chunk of plaster out of my pocket to have another look at the loot. Even in the unsatisfactory mixed light of electricity and dawn, the gem sparkled with a light of its own.

Gerry noticed it and shuddered abruptly. "Get rid of that thing! Diamonds are nothing but bad luck, I promise you. Once they know you've got them, someone's always trying to get them away from you."

I knew what he meant, of course. He meant that none of his birds would ever give him a moment's peace if they knew Perkins & Tate had a diamond lying around loose. For Gerry, that was bad luck enough.

But other people would do a lot to get diamonds, too. How many did Paula have stashed away in that phony cast? Enough to make it worthwhile hijacking her? Had Carrie and her roommate discovered some plot to kidnap Paula and all the jewels she was amassing to bring back to the States illicitly? Was that why they had to be got rid of?

I lapsed into a brief fantasy, starring Tony Christopher and Marie Manzetti as Mafia henchmen assigned to the task. It was hard going—they were too respectable. That was the trouble with the whole tour; everyone was so eminently respectable that it was difficult to realise what they'd been up to. They made one feel that such little lapses could happen to anyone. So, why not hijacking?

As I thought about it, I realised it was the kind of idea you can only get in the cold, gray light of dawn. For one thing, kidnapping Paula would be like trying to kidnap Niagara Falls—how would you impose your will on such a force of nature? And what would you do with it if you got it? For another thing, it would be easier to let her take the jewels through U.S. Customs and steal them later. Even if Paula knew who had taken her jewelry, she couldn't do anything about it—not if she had smuggled it into the States. She would still be liable for all the penalties if she admitted it. There wasn't enough risk in the project for any would-be thief to commit murder over. If there were any such project at all.

I was loathe to relinquish the idea completely. Such was the mesmeric effect of the jewel in my hand. Diamonds were so valuable . . . diamonds were forever . . . diamonds were a girl's best—

"Get rid of it!" Gerry urged. "We don't need any more bad luck. We can get into trouble enough on our own."

He was right, I supposed. I began to realise that it might not be so easy to get rid of. They were funny about things like Customs duty in this country, too. Any reputable jeweler would ask questions—it wouldn't be so easy to sell.

Penny moved to set her coffee cup down on the sofa table behind her. I caught the sudden sharp intake of breath as she turned, and the telltale way her hand crept to her bruised ribs. In the brightening light, I could see that what I had taken to be a shadow on her chin was a blotchy purple bruise. She had put in a lot of overtime on this assignment, and collected nothing but aches and pains for it. There were bonuses and bonuses, and some things girls tended to prize above money.

"Here." I tossed the diamond into her lap—carefully, so that she wouldn't have to move to catch it. "Souvenir of a job well done."

Gerry nodded agreement. I knew that, like me, he was only thankful that she hadn't a few scars for lasting souvenirs, as well.

"Oh, Douglas!" She looked at me, her eyes outshone the diamond for a moment, then went misty. "Oh, Douglas!"

"A present from Paula," I disclaimed hastily, something in her attitude bringing on an acute attack of nervousness.

Pandora paused in washing her face and looked across at Penny. Their eyes met, and an unreadable, completely female, feline message passed between them. Then Pandora went back to washing her face. It gave me the unreasonable feeling that something about my fate had irrevocably been decided, and I had no say in the matter whatever.

"It's all right," Penny said, "I understand. Thank you, Douglas. And"—she turned her head cautiously—"thank you, Gerald."

It was Gerry's turn to jump nervously at this point. It was the first time Penny had ever used our first names. Of course, after what she'd been through, she was entitled to. But it meant the former relationship had changed, was assuming a new and slightly different, unknown form. It had been silly of us to assume that it would remain static forever. As I'd noticed before, Penny was growing up. In fact, the kind of clients we'd been drawing recently were enough to age anyone rapidly. I was feeling a lot older myself.

Pandora finished making herself what she considered presentable and leaped for my shoulder, settling down for a nap. Penny sat curled quietly in the corner of the sofa, gazing into the depths of her jewel, turning it to catch the light, a dreamy smile on her lips. Gerry had gone off into some dream of his own.

It was too early to do anything, too late to go to bed. Soon Neil and the professor would be returning with their grim tidings. Then the police would take over. It would be a few hours before we knew whether we could unload Tour 79 at Heathrow, or whether we were stuck with them for an indefinitely longer period. Meanwhile, there was nothing to do but sit around and wait.

Hotel rooms are notoriously poor at providing reading material. Once you have read the menu—down to the fine print that lets you know that room service has shut off long before you want it, so it's all academic, anyway—and the notices that disclaim all responsibility for valuables unless deposited in the hotel safe, you've had it. Nor was this the sort of hotel to shelter a Gideon Bible. Here, it would be a Gutenberg or nothing. Since the cost of providing a Gutenberg Bible for every room was prohibitive, it was nothing.

Listlessly, I picked up the exercise book. Once I'd removed the two empty and well-licked half slices of bread, it didn't show much indication of Pandora's lunch. I brushed away a couple of crumbs and opened the book idly. "The Trials and Travails of Tour 79"—the trials and travails of Perkins & Tate was more like it.

At least, they'd started out having a good time. I was glad to see that there was nothing but praise for Larkin's Luxury Tours and all the arrangements that had been made for Tour 79. I flipped casually through the notebook, dipping in here and there.

I found the shopping sequence in Amsterdam that Paula had been so worried about. It seemed pretty innocuous to me—a clear case of the guilty fleeing when there was no pursuit. I was interested to notice that some play was made about Carrie's comments on the occasion, however. She seemed to be showing signs of a sharpening temper—perhaps she was just a poor traveler. If she had been, it would be the sort of thing Tris Tablor wouldn't want to admit to himself, since he'd induced her to sign on for the trip.

And then, the last item. A scrawl, the handwriting barely recognisable as by the same hand as that which had gone before: *Why, Carrie, why?*

After that, nothing. Either Tris Tablor had been too broken up to write any more in his journal, or else that was the point at which Paula had managed to "borrow" it.

I closed the notebook and sat staring at it, wondering just what it was about it that had unsettled me so. There was something teasing at the corner of my mind, but I couldn't quite catch the thought.

Then the tap sounded at the door. A perfunctory warning rap immediately before the door opened. It was just as well no one was doing anything they oughtn't—as a warning, it was a washout.

Neil Larkin came into the room, followed by Professor Tablor. It was a toss-up which of them looked worse. Tablor, by a short head, I decided. But then, he was older, had been under a longer-continuing strain, and was ill to begin with.

Instinctively, I struggled to my feet and measured the distance to my briefcase. If Tris Tablor showed any signs of collapsing, I could make it with another standing broad jump. At the moment, however, he seemed to be holding up.

"How is everything?" Neil asked.

"Kate's asleep," I told him. "You might as well let her

rest as long as she can. She had a hard day yesterday. You could do with some rest yourself."

"Couldn't I just!" He shuddered, then remembered his responsibilities to his clients and turned to the professor.

"Why don't you go back and try for some sleep?" Neil suggested. "The police won't be along for a while yet. They can talk to you last. That ought to let you get some rest."

"Rest . . . ," Tris Tablor said dazedly. "Yes . . . rest." He really was looking terrible.

"It was her, then?" I asked.

Neil nodded. "Pulled out of the Thames. She'd been in several days. Since she first disappeared, they think."

"Another . . . suicide?"

"Probably." He looked at me warily. "That will be for the police to decide, won't it? They'll be along later; they'll give everyone a chance to have breakfast first." He grimaced. "We're getting kid-glove treatment—they're probably hoping they can handle this without anyone's screaming for the American Embassy."

"I can see that it would complicate matters," I said. Delay them, too, but there was no use in pointing that out. Neil knew it as well as I did.

But Professor Tablor was worrying both of us. He stood there, shaking his head slightly, like a punch-drunk fighter. "It goes on," he said vaguely. "It keeps going on. One thing leads to another. Isn't there ever an end?"

"Come on, Professor." Neil took his arm firmly. "Rest. There's nothing more you can do."

I walked to the door with them. As they were leaving, I held out the exercise book to Tris Tablor. He took it, staring at it for a moment as though he didn't recognise it. Then he raised his head and looked at me questioningly.

"It just . . . turned up," I said. "The way things do. It got mixed up with someone else's luggage. The way things do."

As an explanation, it was so feeble it was helpless, but he accepted it. Nodding his head, as though he understood all about the way these mysterious things can happen, he tucked it under his arm with the small package he was carrying.

Neil was tugging at him, but he remained in the doorway a moment longer, staring at me. "It can't keep going on," he said intensely. "It's got to end sometime. It's got to."

"It will." I tried to be encouraging. "Soon."

"Soon." He nodded, catching at the word as though it were a promise. "Soon." Neil was pulling at his arm again, and this time, he responded. The door closed behind them.

Penny and Gerry were both half-dozing now, Penny still clutching her precious chunk of plaster like a child with a toy on Christmas night. Except that a diamond was a lot more valuable than any toy.

Valuable. My mind refused to rest and sent me pacing the room. Different people had different values. I wondered what Donna's values would be, in future years. She was just about old enough to repudiate Paula and everything Paula held sacred. Whatever she turned to, it wouldn't be diamonds.

Outside, the day had arrived. Charladies waited in bus queues, homeward bound after a night of cleaning office blocks. Overeager desk workers walked briskly toward their offices and another day's labours.

Perhaps I had dozed off, too, asleep on my feet. Suddenly, without any awareness on my part of the passage of time, it was a lot later than I thought it could be. That was what came of not having anything to concentrate your attention on. Of having nothing to read.

For a brief moment, I regretted returning Tris Tablor's

notebook to him so promptly. I could have kept it awhile longer, he wouldn't have minded, he had written it for others to read. True, it hadn't made such scintillating reading, but he was a professor of physics, not literature.

Physics. Suddenly, it came flooding back to me. He had said Carrie's protégé had believed he had evolved a new theory—one that Tris Tablor had torn to pieces. Yet later, Tablor had announced that *he* was publishing an exciting new theory in the autumn—eighteen months after Carrie's protégé had "committed suicide."

But Carrie had been the boy's mentor and friend. She would most probably have seen his physics thesis—he would have shown it to her—perhaps asked her criticism on the writing—she was an English professor. She would recognise it if she read it again. And if the same thesis was appearing soon under Tablor's name, she would inevitably see it, recognise it, question it . . .

But Carrie had providentially "committed suicide" in Switzerland. It was Tris Tablor who had told me that about the woman's death. Insisted on it. Another suicide.

Then Angela Hunt, who had been Carrie's roommate on the tour, to whom she might have confided something, speculated about something—who just might have known something about those pills she was or wasn't taking—had died here in London. And Tablor had claimed that he had put her into the taxi to catch the train. He had been the last to see her alive. The police were sure to follow up on that.

"*It keeps happening,*" Tris Tablor had just been saying. As he had said earlier, "*Sometimes people commit suicide by forcing other people to kill them.*" As neat a piece of rationalisation as I had ever encountered—it was too bad I hadn't recognised it for what it was at the time. When he had looked at his betraying, murderous hands as though he had never seen them before. As though they had an independent life of their own that he was powerless to control.

Also, his expression that night in the pub had been so peculiar as to be frightening. He must have heard Winnie and Billie Mae confiding in me—he'd been close enough to overhear. He had covered it by diverting my attention to Pandora, but he must have been facing a crisis then. Facing just how long it could go on, how far it could go. He was fundamentally a quiet, basically conscientious scholar who had been pushed beyond his limits, succumbed to temptation, and then had had to kill to cover up. But he couldn't keep on killing—too many people were involved. He wasn't the stuff mass murderers are made of.

And he had said, tonight, *"It's got to end . . . soon."* The shape of that package under his arm reminded me of something else he had said earlier as well. *"For her to sit there and eat that cheese fondue was as much an act of suicide as it would be for me to eat my way through . . ."*

I gave a shout that brought Gerry to his feet, snatched up my briefcase, and rushed for the door. I couldn't wait for the lift—I took the stairs two at a time.

I banged on Tablor's door, but there was no answer. I had hardly expected any, but I went on trying.

"What's the matter?" Gerry came up behind me, ashen. "What's got into you?"

I began kicking the door, but a chambermaid hurried up with a master key before I could do any damage. She inserted the key into the lock, turned it, and swung the door open, looking at me as though she thought I had lost my senses, but was afraid I hadn't. Word about the guests and their problems circulates quickly behind the scenes. I started forward slowly.

"*Aaaraayow!*" With a wail of distress, Pandora dropped to the floor from my shoulder and crouched there.

"Come on." I stooped and tried to pick her up. Still wailing faintly, she dug her claws into the carpet and refused to be budged. Quivering, wailing, she refused to cross that threshold. I knew then, if I hadn't known before.

I straightened up and walked slowly into Professor Tablor's room. The others grouped together in the doorway behind me, as though afraid of what they might discover if they followed me. But there was nothing dramatic to be seen.

There was only a trail of empty candy wrappers across the carpet, leading to the huddled, motionless form on the bed.

ABOUT THE AUTHOR

MARIAN BABSON has written over twenty mystery novels. Most recently, her many readers are being treated to a series, of which *Tourists Are for Trapping* is the third. Babson is an American who for many years has made her home in London.

If you enjoyed TOURISTS ARE FOR TRAPPING, you will enjoy Marian Babson's next Perkins & Tate mystery, COVER-UP STORY, which will be published in November of 1991.

The following is a preview of the suspenseful mystery, COVER-UP STORY.

CHAPTER I

THE PRESS CONFERENCE was going well—as Press Conferences go. The Fleet Street boys were lit up, the Client wasn't. Their initial efforts to trap him into some incautious quotations had been sidestepped and they were past caring now. His latest LP was booming out over the amplifiers with a hypnotic beat, and the Press Release was so well written—if I do say it myself—that any sub could dredge a few hundred salient words out of it when his principal staggered back to the office.

For the moment, it looked as though I could relax. I snatched a Martini as the tray went past and retreated into a corner where I could keep an eye peeled for trouble.

It was the wrong corner and trouble was waiting

for me. 'That room you got for Lou-Ann—' Maw Cooney had been lurking behind the drapes—'won't do at all. I never saw such a poky little hole in all my born days. Are you sure this is a high-class hotel?'

I took a deep swallow before replying. She'd done nothing but complain since she stepped off the boat-train. 'It's generally considered to be one of the best hotels in London.'

'I'd hate to see the worst!' She sniffed and glanced sharply at the glass in my hand. 'Young man, are you supposed to be drinking on duty?'

'I'm a Public Relations Officer, Mrs Cooney—not a policeman.' To underline this, I took another swallow. You have to assert your independence with some of these characters. And she wasn't paying my salary.

'You haven't answered me. What about Lou-Ann? The Good Lord knows I don't mind for myself—I could sleep on a heap of rags in a corner—but it's a question of the fitness of things. Lou-Ann *is* the comedy star of this Troupe, after all, and it's mighty kind of her to agree to double up with her dresser—but to ask *two* of us to share that teensy little—'

'I'll see what I can do, Mrs Cooney,' I interrupted her. 'In fact, I'll see right now.' I got away quickly before she could block my retreat.

This corner was an improvement. There was nobody here but us chickens. It was clear now that the crowd was beginning to thin out a bit.

The LP hesitated, then began on the big one—the Top of the Charts—the number that had lifted Our Boy right out of the boondocks and into the big time.

'Homesteader, Homesteader,
    'Ridin' alone . . .'

You could call it Ballad, Country & Western, or Folk Music—whatever was 'in' this year. The music was plaintive, the lyric melancholy—and it had touched a chord in a lot of people. It was about a homesteader who had fenced off his acres, then had to fight beef barons who reckoned they owned the grazing rights to every acre of God's whole creation; just as he was wearying of the struggle, they cut a hole in his fence and stampeded the cattle through; his wife and the child she was about to bear were killed, and now they'd never drive him away because all he had was buried here on this homestead, and he'd stay until they buried him here, too. The Client was alleged to have written it himself—and it sounded semi-literate enough to be possible.

'Homesteader, Homesteader,
    'Ridin' alone . . .'

Uncle No'ccount moved forward slowly, pulling his harmonica and a red bandana from his hip pocket. He spat his upper teeth into the bandana and stowed it back in his pocket. He wrapped his lips around the harmonica and breathed into it. A cold wail of melody whiffled a chill down every spine as he picked up the tune.

He was every bum who'd ever hopped a midnight

freight, one jump ahead of the railroad police, on his way from nowhere to nowhere, gone too long from home to even remember what he was running from any more.

'Ridin' alone now,

'For ever alone . . .'

Cousin Homer chimed in softly with the guitar and Cousin Ezra took up the plaint with the fiddle. They seemed okay, although a bit too awkward and gangly, with wrists and ankles dangling too far out of their clothing for their ages. If they'd done any growing since they bought those clothes, they ought to will their bodies to the Harvard School of Pathology. Still, the fans hadn't seemed to notice—and who was I to knock a successful routine?

They were all playing along with the record now. If the Client held out much longer, it was going to be pointed. I looked over to try to catch his eye.

I needn't have bothered. He was already moving front and centre, grinning his lazy grin, forelock down over one eye, gliding with easy catlike grace. The grin didn't reach his eyes. The reluctance in his shrug was real—the self-deprecation wasn't. I'd only known this crew for six hours, but already I had enough of the picture to realize that there was going to be hell to pay for this performance—after the Press had left.

They'd reached the echo chamber bit when he took up the tempo. He looked more like Black Bart the Last of the Bushwhackers than Bart the Lonely

Homesteader; but this was the act that was paying off, so this was the act he was doing—or almost.

The echo chamber did a little to disguise it, the live music did the rest, but Black Bart wasn't singing. His timing was perfect, the graceful throwaway gestures fitted perfectly. He stood there, miming to the record and, except for the musicians, I was probably the only one to notice it. It confirmed my opinion. The Client wasn't giving anything away free.

'Homesteader, Homesteader,
      'For ever alone . . .'

The spattering of applause showed how far the party had gone towards breaking up. During the number the waiters had been moving around purposefully, removing empty glasses from tables and detaching near-empty glasses from hands. Ashtrays were being emptied, and a couple of old-retainer types were doddering forward from the far end of the room, managing, like ancient collies, to herd the strays along in front of them.

The Client patted a few shoulders as they passed. 'Nice to have met y'all,' he said. 'Sure hope I'll be seeing a lot more of you.'

His eye had been resting on someone's little office junior as he said that, and I got a nasty feeling that it had a double meaning. At the very least. We were being paid far too much for this job—there must be some deep jagged icebergs beneath the glittering tops that broke the surface.

The last of the Press, exiting, collided with Lou-

Ann, entering. She squawked and hurled herself back against the door frame. They glanced at her curiously, but Crystal Harper was right behind her, and nobody with all their hormones operational was going to waste time looking at Lou-Ann when Crystal was around.

Maw Cooney swept down on Lou-Ann, scolding, 'Where've you been? All them reporters were here—and they were taking pictures, too. Now you've missed the whole thing. And you, the comedy star!'

'Sorry, Maw,' Crystal Harper said, with lazy indifference, 'I'm afraid we went shopping and didn't notice the time. Girls will be girls, you know.'

Maw Cooney flashed her a look that told her she'd never been a girl. Several unmentionable variations, perhaps, but never *that* kind of girl.

Over Maw's head, Crystal met the Client's eyes. *He* wasn't complaining. It occurred to me that it might have been deliberately engineered that Lou-Ann miss the Press Reception.

Lou-Ann whirled around and began babbling apologies to the Client. He nodded, not really looking at her. 'It don't matter. You're all right, honey.'

'But I missed *everything*. Now they won't have any pictures of me,' she wailed.

'You go talk to the Publicity Boy,' the Client jerked a thumb at me. 'He'll fix up something. That's what we're paying him for.' He gave her a shove that was rough but—for him—probably not unkindly, and she stumbled towards me.

*   *   *

She was the kid next door who had grown up, taken the braces off her teeth, thrown away her glasses, had her hair curled—and then found out that it *still* didn't make any difference. So she'd decided to play it for laughs. Sometimes they make worse decisions.

Somewhere between the shopping tour and the Press Reception, she'd climbed into her trade mark 'comedy costume'. The high-necked long-sleeved blouse bunched itself out of a low-necked short-sleeved red jacket with half the buttons missing. The rusty black skirt dipped to several lengths and multi-coloured patches had been sewn at random on it. The straw hat had two large daisies drooping from broken stalks and was moored precariously to the top of her head by an elastic string passed under her braids.

The freckles scattered all over her face were probably real and not painted on. She smiled at me nervously. There was lipstick on her front teeth. I didn't think that was an intentional part of the costume— she was just the sort who always would have lipstick on her front teeth.

'I'm sorry,' she said. I had to lean forward to hear her. 'I should have kept an eye on the time, but it was so excitin' bein' here, and seeing all those famous stores—'

'Don't you go apologizing to *him*—he should apologize to *you*.' Maw Cooney had come up behind us with the battleflag flying. 'You're paying him—it was his job to keep those reporters here until you arrived. Stars are *expected* to be late. How dare he start before you got here?'

Lou-Ann looked up at me. She'd been chewing gum. Now she pursed her lips suddenly and broke into a broad grin, goggling her eyes at me. It was liquorice gum, and she'd blacked out her two front teeth. On the whole, I preferred the lipstick.

But I recognized it as another form of apology, this time for Maw Cooney, so I nodded and smiled at her, and she relaxed.

Over her shoulder, there was a performance going on in the second ring.

Black Bart had come up behind the musicians as they were settling down their instruments. When Uncle No'ccount pulled the bandana containing his upper set from his pocket, Bart snatched it away.

'You stupid no-account old fool!' He balled his massive fist around the bandana and shook it under Uncle No'ccount's nose. 'What do you think you're playing at? Know what I ought to do? I ought to stomp on these for you!'

'Aw, now, Bart, don't take on so.' Uncle No'ccount kept his eyes on his uppers. 'We didn't mean no harm.'

'You never mean no harm—but you go and do it just the same. Listen, when I decide we'll do a Benefit, *I'll* give the word!'

'Sure, Bart, sure. I just got kinda carried away. Didn't mean to upset you none—did we, boys?'

The Cousins shuffled their feet and shook their heads, miserable at being appealed to. Only too obviously, they had been hoping to remain unnoticed and escape involvement.

'We was just funning, Bart.'

'No call to take on like that, Bart.' They spoke together, backing towards the door.

''Tweren't like a for-real show, anyhow, Bart,' Cousin Ezra said. 'You know we ain't wired up right yet for this neck of the woods.'

'That's right, Bart,' Cousin Homer chipped in. 'That fella there said he was gonna see about it, but he ain't done nothing yet.'

That sent the ball swinging into my court.

'You, boy!' Black Bart shouted at me. 'Hump it over here and let's hear what you got to say for yourself. How come you ain't got my boys fixed up yet?'

Uncle No'ccount reached out and gently removed his belongings from Bart's hand while he was distracted. A quick flourish of the bandana and his teeth were firmly where they ought to be. He beamed with relief and straightened his shoulders, standing taller.

'Reckon I'd better get along and tend to some unpacking,' he said. 'You don't need me for this. One thing about a good old harmonica—you cain't fit wires to it.'

'Okay, but you just watch it, you hear?' Bart glared, but the menace was wasted on Uncle No'ccount's back, so he turned it on me.

'You don't move very fast round these parts, do you, boy? We told you as soon as we got here an' took a look at the electricity to get the plugs changed an' slap transformers on all the instruments. S'pose I shouldn't be surprised it ain't been done yet, now I see how long it takes you to even cross a room.'

It was a pity Perkins & Tate (Public Relations) Ltd needed the money so badly. It would have been a pleasure to tell him what I thought of him and walk out.

On second thought, I probably couldn't tell him anything he hadn't heard before. And we needed the money. He might be a bastard, but he was a solvent bastard.

'I put in a call for an electrician,' I said. 'They promised to speed it up and have one over here first thing in the morning. That means some time tomorrow afternoon.'

He glared at me suspiciously, but seemed to realize I was serious. 'Hell! What a country!' he exploded. 'I got thousands of dollars worth of electronic equipment here, and it ain't worth a damn unless I can get the juice going through it.'

'You'll have everything ready in time for your opening,' I said. 'You've only been in the country about eight hours, why not relax and enjoy it?'

'You trying to be smart, boy?'

'We had to skimp the introductions to get ready for the Press,' I said. 'My name is Perkins, Douglas Perkins.'

'Like I said, you trying to be smart, *boy*?'

The Cousins began to snicker, then to push each other about. 'You hear that, *boy*? Yes, sir, *boy*!' They scuffled wildly.

'All right, cut that out!' They had brought unwelcome attention back to themselves. 'You got off light—*this time*. Don't let it go to your heads.'

'Yeah, Bart.' 'Sure, Bart.' They were instantly subdued.

'You got nothing better to do—cut along to your hotel and get some more practice. You flatted that top note on me. Do that on stage and you'll be swimming back home the hard way—under water.'

They slunk away quietly, but before I had time to enjoy the peace, Maw Cooney was on us.

'Young man, have you got that room changed yet? By rights, we ought to have a suite. You can't expect Lou-Ann to put up with being treated like poor white trash.'

Since that was what she'd gone to great trouble to dress herself up to look like, it would seem to be an occupational hazard. Perhaps that was why Maw Cooney, as her dresser, was so sensitive about it.

'*You* tell him,' she whirled on Bart. 'Lou-Ann is the comedy star of this Troupe. She deserves better than that poky old room. There isn't room enough to swing a cat in there. Tell him we want a room befitting her position.'

You had to hand it to her for bravery, if not sheer gall. They were lucky to be in the same hotel as the Great Bart. Uncle No'ccount and the Cousins had been salted away over in the heart of 'Europe On Five Dollars A Day' territory. But, obviously, Maw Cooney was not one to sit back and count her blessings.

Bart turned his head slowly to stare down at her. I closed my eyes. I hate to see a man hit an old lady—no matter how much she's been asking for it.

When I opened them, she was still standing there, untouched. Bart's eyes had narrowed dangerously, but he hadn't said a word.

'You tell him now.' She insisted on crowding her luck. 'You order him to find a nicer room for Lou-Ann. You know it's due her—in her position.'

Crystal had moved up behind Bart and, once again, an unspoken communication passed between them.

Suddenly, Bart shrugged. 'Right, Maw.' He glared at me. 'See to it, boy!' He jerked his head at Crystal and they left the room together.

Maw Cooney fussed her way back to collect Lou-Ann. On their way out, she stopped to say, 'We'll pack our things. We didn't unpack much, anyhow, once we saw that awful place. You get the bellboy to move us. We'll be out getting a bite to eat.'

I stared after them thoughtfully. After a moment, a throat being cleared over by the door brought me back to the scene.

BANTAM MYSTERY COLLECTION

- 24958 **DEATH OF A GHOST** Allingham $3.95
- 28506 **POLICE AT FUNERAL** Allingham $3.95
- 28073 **JEMIMA SHORE'S FIRST CASE** Fraser $3.95
- 28071 **A SPLASH OF RED** Fraser $3.95
- 28096 **MURDER SAILS AT MIDNIGHT** Babson $3.50
- 28061 **MANHATTAN IS MY BEAT** Deaver $3.95
- 28070 **OXFORD BLOOD** Fraser $3.95
- 27663 **THE RAIN** Peterson $3.95
- 28019 **YOUR ROYAL HOSTAGE** Fraser $3.95
- 28590 **MURDER AT THE CAT SHOW** Babson $3.95
- 28495 **THE DA VINCI DECEPTION** Swan $4.95
- 27860 **THE SCARRED MAN** Peterson $4.50
- 28824 **CUPID** Reid $3.95
- 28044 **SAN FRANCISCO KILLS** Flinn $3.95
- 28816 **FUSE TIME** Byrd $4.95
- 18512 **HOT WIRE** Russell $2.50
- 28926 **BLIND SPOT** Russell $3.95
- 28311 **QUIET AS A NUN** Fraser $4.50

Bantam Books, Dept. MC, 414 East Golf Road, Des Plaines, IL 60016

Please send me the items I have checked above. I am enclosing $_____
(please add $2.50 to cover postage and handling). Send check or money
order, no cash or C.O.D.s please.

Mr/Ms _____

Address _____

City/State_____ Zip _____

MC-4/91

Please allow four to six weeks for delivery.
Prices and availability subject to change without notice.